PENGUIN METRO READS

HOUSE OF STARS

Keya Ghosh retired early as an English teacher at a girls' school in the hills. Tired of confiscating trashy romance novels from her students, which 'did nothing for either their idea of adult relationships or their ability to write English', she decided to take up the challenge of reinventing the chick-lit novel. She is working on a trio of novels in the calm environs of the Velliangiri mountains. Her early retirement also allows her to pursue her hobby of tracing the lost works of the early female Bhakti poets. *Terror@Twelve*, her collection of urban ghost stories, was published by Juggernaut.

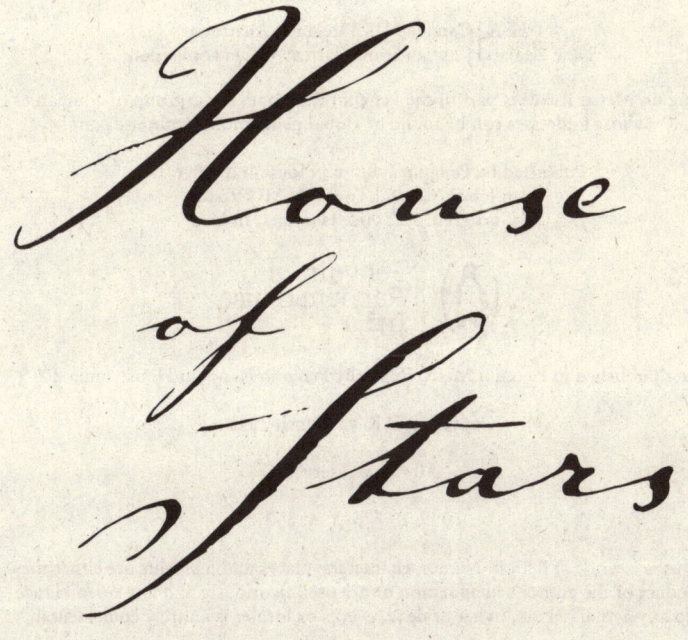

KEYA GHOSH

Penguin
metro reads

An imprint of Penguin Random House

PENGUIN METRO READS

USA | Canada | UK | Ireland | Australia
New Zealand | India | South Africa | China | Singapore

Penguin Metro Reads is part of the Penguin Random House group of companies
whose addresses can be found at global.penguinrandomhouse.com

Published by Penguin Random House India Pvt. Ltd
4th Floor, Capital Tower 1, MG Road,
Gurugram 122 002, Haryana, India

First published in Penguin Metro Reads by Penguin Random House India 2019

ISBN 9780143447351

Typeset in Adobe Garamond Pro by Manipal Digital Systems, Manipal

Printed at Repro India Limited

www.penguin.co.in

This is a legitimate digitally printed version of the book and therefore might not
have certain extra finishing on the cover.

Dearest K,
You taught me that love lasts beyond death.
You are and always will be the love that
transmuted my life and filled it with light.

House of Stars

Kabir

Damn. She is beautiful.

I have been following her for three days, and this is the first time that I really see her. She stands hesitantly on the stairs. A breeze lifts the hair off her face. And she is beautiful.

Aman crows in my ear, 'I told you. You thought I was just boasting about my girlfriend!'

The photo he had shown me was of a group of people. She was just an uncertain figure hiding at the right edge. She had turned her face away at the moment that the photo was taken, so all the camera got was her long hair and a side profile. But her beauty had been apparent in his voice when he spoke of her. 'She's got this long hair that falls absolutely straight. She never ties it up. And her eyes . . . *yaar* . . . so gentle. You can fall right into them.'

Her hair falls straight, except when the wake of passing cars ripples it away from her face. Her face is tiny and

1

heart-shaped. I cannot see her eyes from across the road. But I want to.

I stare at her through the curtain of traffic that roars between us. Aman jerks me into action. 'Hurry! You'll lose her,' he says insistently in my ear.

I hurry after her. My heart is thumping. I stick my hands in the pockets of my jeans to stop them trembling. Just the thought of going up to a girl and talking to her does that to me. I'm a loser in the girl department. Can't be helped. I haven't had much practice.

For three days, I've been standing outside the gate of the fancy college that Aman used to go to. He had pointed her out to me the first day. All I ever got was a glimpse of a girl in jeans and a kurta who slipped out of an expensive car and hurried into the college, head down. Same thing when it was time to go home. Three days of waiting, and that was all. But this morning, that changes. She hurries through the gate after the car drops her off. But after it drives away, she comes back out hesitantly. And I finally see the girl who had been described to me in poetry.

She gets an auto. I manage to grab an auto too. When I tell the driver to follow her, he has a lot to say. Smart-ass, like all Mumbai rickshaw drivers are. '*Pyaar vyaar ka chakkar hai?*' I ignore him.

'You'll end up in trouble,' he prophesies. 'All women and love are trouble.'

She stops the auto at a large mall. I have to crane my neck to look up at it. Biggest damn thing I've ever seen. A huge facade of glass in which my shabby self stands reflected, gaping like a fool.

I hurry through the entrance after her. The security guards stop me and do a cursory pat-down. I could tell them that I am carrying everything I possess in the world. And it isn't much.

The shops in the mall are still in the process of opening. Shutters clatter, an automatic sweeper wheezes around the floor. The mall is three storeys high, with escalators stretching their long necks like mechanical giraffes between floors. Fancy names glitter in chrome and crystal and neon from the entryways. It's one of those premium places where you can buy anything, from diamond jewellery to home theatre systems, and everything else in between.

She doesn't seem to be interested in any of the shops, walking past them without looking and heading straight to an escalator.

'Give her the letter,' says Aman. 'You promised you'd do that for me. Go on.'

I had made him that promise. And I have come such a long distance to keep it. And I mean to, even though my heart jolts when she turns her head and I see her for the first time. God. She is beautiful.

'I can't get close to her.'

'Oh, come on. You haven't come all this way to give up now. You owe me this. Remember?'

I remember all right. I owe him this. I watched him write the letter in the light of a lamp. Thinking over every word. Knowing these might be the last words she ever heard from him. I watched him fold it carefully. His love letter lies warm against my heart. I can't help but wish it were mine.

3

I follow her around the mall. She goes in and out of shops, then wanders into a large department store and walks through the various sections. I trail behind her, trying to be unobtrusive. The salesgirls keep a nervous eye on me, this shabby, unkempt boy wandering around their pristine fancy displays. I can see them watching my hands, dreading that I will reach out and touch something.

We go through the make-up section, and the place where they keep ladies' kurtas, dresses, T-shirts. At the handbags section I finally summon up enough courage.

I edge closer to her, trying to work up the nerve to tap her on the shoulder, to actually touch her.

This is it. I'm actually going to talk to a girl. I clear my throat.

She doesn't notice. She has turned and is walking rapidly away. I follow, holding on to the courage I have mustered. She pushes through a door, and I grit my teeth and almost follow, when I read the sign on it—'Ladies'. I stop dead, all my momentum draining out of me.

She is in there a long time. Long enough for me to worry. Long enough for me to wonder if something is wrong, if I should push open the door and check. When the door finally slams open, I am unprepared, and she steps out straight into my stare.

She looks at me, and her eyes are red, as if she has been crying. Then, before I can say a word, she turns and hurries away. I hurry after her, but she is almost running.

At the top of the escalator, she abruptly turns and confronts me. 'Who are you? Why are you following me?'

I fumble for an answer. Before I can say a word, she shouts, 'Guard! Security! This man is harassing me!'

There is a security guard nearby who turns at her call. Then he seems to fold and falls gently to the ground, at our feet. There is a sharp chatter of sound at the entrance. I know that sound. It's three quick bursts from an AK-47. She is standing there, staring at the guard in shock. I don't stop to think. I fling myself on her.

One moment too scared to lay a finger on her, the next minute my arms and legs and body are entangled with hers. She turns a frightened and furious face to me, and I cover her mouth before she can scream. 'Please. I'm sorry. Just lie still!' I beg. And the world descends into chaos.

A group of men run into the mall. They have guns. People begin screaming. Guns begin firing.

I lie there, heart thundering, adrenaline rushing through me, brain screaming that I should get out of there. I don't dare move.

I am aware of everything all at once. She is soft and startlingly warm. A lemony scent wafts from her hair. Her skin smells of flowers. The curve of her ear is brown and pink and almost touches my lips. Her bangles are sharp stripes against my arm. I'll tell you this—it's strange and awkward to be lying on her, but I don't want to move. She is frozen in shock, eyes wide and fixed on me. I see the understanding come into them that I am not attacking her. She has recognized the sounds at last.

One me is lost. Another me is coldly watching and calculating everything else. I listen intently, sorting out sounds from the crescendo of panic. Five men. Three automatics. One handgun.

The mall security guys don't wait. They're out of the door, shoving customers out of their way. The gunmen run through the mall, searching for exits; securing them. Their guns spit non-stop. Sometimes as a warning, sometimes meaning business.

I watch an old man fall to the ground. His blood pools and meanders in slow streams across the floor towards the entrance. A screaming woman slips in it and falls. She scrabbles hysterically in the blood for a second, before she gets back on her feet and runs. Others are scrambling for the doors as well. Then two gunmen head to the entrance and begin stopping them.

It's all over in about ten minutes. A gunman stops beside us. She clutches me and closes her eyes. I cover as much of her as I can. If there are going to be bullets, I might as well take them. No one is going to notice I'm gone.

'What, *saale*?' says the man, kicking me in the thigh. 'Protecting your girl? Being a bloody hero? Get up!'

His gun is cold against my temple. I get up. I have to take her hand and pull her up. She is trembling and icy-cold. Her hand slips out of mine. I wish I could keep holding it. She stumbles on to the escalator ahead of me. I look around for Aman.

When the shooting is over, we're part of a group of hostages huddled miserably in the middle of the foyer. Aman is gone.

Diya

I hate my father. He has never ever asked me what I want before making a decision about my life. I remember when I was just four years old and there was a fancy-dress competition at the playschool I went to. I wanted with all my heart to go as a princess. My mother had bought the crown and everything. But the night before the competition, my father said, 'She will go as Mother India.' Just what every little girl dreams of being. Mother India. I cried and cried. He slapped me to get me to stop.

This morning, my father announced at breakfast that it was time I got married and that he was looking for a suitable match. My mother said nothing. She never does.

I knew this would happen some day. I was prepared and raised my head. 'I'm just in SYJC. I'm below the legal age for marriage. You can't do that.'

'Can't do that?' my father said. 'And who is going to stop me?'

Nobody can. That is the thing I've learnt since I've been old enough to walk. My mother learnt it even earlier. After twenty-two years of marriage, he's got her well-trained. He is the law in our house. The judge. And the sentence is obedience at any cost.

I know him. He'll choose someone who will want me well-trained too. I won't be my mother. I won't! I love her. I feel sorry for her. But I won't be her.

I didn't argue. I put my head down and went on with breakfast. My mother didn't even look at me. I tried to think of what to do.

I wanted to run away, but there was nowhere to go. Not a single person or place that would give me shelter. I desperately needed to think. So I came to the mall. I like empty malls. They belong to no one. People drift in and out of shops trying to buy happiness, and, with a bag or two in their hands, I see them smile. I've got enough money. But it has never bought me happiness.

I first notice someone following me when I walk through the kurta section. He just walks past the displays. Doesn't stop to look at anything. And why would he look at kurtas for women, anyway? I go from there to the women's casuals section to check, and sure enough, he walks in behind me.

He's a teenage boy. Tall and very fair, but with shabby, crumpled clothes and hair that has not been combed. Jeans. Faded T-shirt. He slips along behind me, trying to be nonchalant. I study him in a mirror, pretending to look at jewellery. I go to the bathroom to buy a little time. To wait and see.

When I come out, there he is. My heart begins to thud. He doesn't look like one of the men sent by my father to watch me. He's too young. Too shabby. Maybe he's just some unknown boy following a girl to harass her. I do the only thing I can think of. I yell for security.

Then he flings himself on top of me.

I can't tell you how scared I am. I panic. He puts his hand over my mouth so I can't scream. I think I'm being assaulted. Then I hear gunshots. Screaming.

I lie under him, not daring to move. I can sense the chaos. People are running, their footsteps thudding wildly. There is hysterical screaming. One woman is shouting again and again, 'Oh God! Oh God!' I hear someone falling heavily to the ground. From the corner of my eye, I see a pool of red seeping from the fallen security guard. I close my eyes.

I don't know who the boy is. I don't know why he's protecting me. But he is all that lies between me and a bullet.

Then the screaming stops. The silence feels even more dangerous. I hear footsteps coming towards us. A man with a gun is yelling at us to get up.

For one second, I want to hold on to this unknown boy. I'm scared and desperate to hold on to anything. But we are separated.

We are told to sit down and wait. There are many of us all huddled together, all numb with shock. No one dares to scream. But there is the sound of subdued crying, the whisper of prayers.

I watch the men with guns. I'm scared of them, but, however stupid this sounds, I'm far more scared of my father finding out that I've gone somewhere without letting him know. The only thought that keeps going through my head is, *He's going to be so angry. So angry.*

Here I am, held hostage by terrorists—blood on the floor, terrified people around me—and all I can think of is what my father is going to say. *Thanks, Dad. You've already done a good job training me.*

A tremendous rattling and screeching sounds through the mall. The metal shutters are being pulled down. The terrorists are closing down the mall. We watch as shutters block out the light from the huge show windows. Only the shutter over the door is left up. It begins to rumble down with a numbing finality. A man steps through before it is halfway. He is an ordinary-looking man. His hair is grey, and he is not very tall. His hands are chained. With a rattle of the chain, he stretches them as far as they will go. 'I thank you, my brothers,' he says.

The terrorists crowd around him, smiles on their faces. A man with a black headband, who seems to be the leader, says, 'We did this almost according to plan. If it hadn't been for the roadroller—'

The grey-haired man raises a hand and the chains jingle. 'We did it almost according to our plan. Perhaps God has something bigger in mind for us. We are part of God's plan now.' He kneels and spreads his hands on the floor. Another terrorist steps forward and presses a gun against the chains. A single retort and his hands are free. He rises, and the men embrace him one by one. There are various expressions on their faces. Pride, respect, outright awe. I don't know who the man is, but he is the power in the room.

The man with the black headband and the grey-haired man confer. Then the rest of the men get their orders. They begin to move among us, asking us our names.

We don't realize what it is for until they begin separating us. Everyone with a Muslim name in one group. Everybody else in another.

Kabir

The terrorists begin to sort people out. Hindus on one side, Muslims on another. We have one Jain among us, but we don't seem to have any Christians. This is not going well.

A shop assistant is hauled up. He says his name is Hussain. But his name tag says 'A. Sharma'. The leader hits him across the face with his gun. His lip splits open, and he struggles to speak with the blood dripping from his mouth. 'It is my name! I work in a designer store. They like us to have suitable names. We can't use our own.'

'Pray,' says the leader. 'Let's see which God you pray to.' In a trembling voice, 'A. Sharma' begins. He is so scared that his voice stutters and shakes. He is barely able to get the words out.

The grey-haired man steps forward and stops him. 'This is no way to speak to God,' he says. 'Not in terror. Calm down. Do not be afraid.'

The boy takes great gasping breaths. The man speaks gently. 'Go, Hussain. Go sit with your brothers.' The boy goes, blood dripping down the front of his shirt.

The person in front of me gets to his feet. He's an old man, and his name is Mahendra Shyam Bhonsle. He shuffles off towards the growing group on the left.

Then it's my turn. I get to my feet but keep my head down. Never make eye contact. It's when you do, that things start to happen. They see you. And madmen like this mostly don't like what they see. From the corner of my eye, I see that I am facing a boy who looks younger than me. He barely has fuzz on his chin, and his eyes dart everywhere.

'What's your name?' he asks.

I say, 'Kabir.'

'Ah. And you are Hindu or Muslim?'

My tongue keeps going without any instructions from my brain. 'My name is Kabir. I was born in an orphanage. I have no idea what I am.'

That catches the attention of the leader in the black headband. He walks over. 'Really? We have ourselves a smart-ass. I could pull your pants down and check.'

I say nothing. He walks around me, inspecting me. I keep my head down. Don't look. Do not catch his eye.

'I think I should just shoot him. Let God sort him out.'

Shit. Shit. Shit.

He gestures with the gun he is holding. 'Get on your knees,' he says.

I do as he says, knowing that I've been really stupid. I should have just given them my name. But I left that name behind some time ago. I don't want to be that person any more. I've run away from that person. I've travelled more than a thousand kilometres to get away.

He puts the gun to my head, but his tone is all nice and friendly. 'Kabir, give me one reason why I shouldn't shoot you. Mother waiting at home? Little sister who loves you?'

I can't think of a thing. 'I'm an orphan,' I mutter.

The grey-haired man speaks up. 'No one is an orphan. We are all God's children. The question is: which God?'

'I don't know,' I say. 'I never cared enough to make a choice.'

'All right then.' The gun is cold against my temple. 'This would be a good time to make a choice.'

I whisper frantically so only he can hear, 'I haven't even lived!'

He leans forward to ask softly, 'Never had a girl?'

'No.'

'Never been kissed?'

'No. I don't want to die before being kissed.'

The gun stays steady on my temple. Then it begins to shake. Black Headband is laughing. 'I doubt you're going to get lucky in our current situation,' he says.

I sense the glance that goes between him and the grey-haired man. Then Black Headband shrugs and lowers the gun. The grey-haired man speaks up. 'Go. Any group. Make the choice you have not made so far.'

I get off my knees to walk back, and stumble and nearly fall. Relief has turned my knees to jelly. I try to walk calmly. I know they are all watching to see which group I will choose.

I have a promise to keep. There is no real choice for me. I walk over to the group that holds her. I sit down with the non-Muslims.

All those with Muslim names head in a group for the exit, their hands on their heads. The shutters are opened 2 feet high. They have to crawl out.

If I had given the right name, I would be on my hands and knees right now heading for freedom. But promises chain you with a bond that even a bullet can't break. The letter rustles against my heart. I lean back and look for her.

She is sitting on the ground, her face hidden by her long hair. She does not look up.

Diya

My name? I can't tell them my name. I just make up another surname. The first thing that comes into my head. Diya Shourie. I realize I have my college ID in my bag. I take it out and shove it up the leg of my churidar. That's all I can think of on the spur of the moment.

They take our mobiles and our bags next. Make us empty our pockets. One well-dressed lady says, 'I simply cannot let you have my handbag. It's brand new and very expensive.'

A man snatches it from her, flings it on the ground, and stamps on it twice. 'Now it isn't,' he says. After that, everyone hurries to hand over whatever they're asked for.

We sit quietly on the floor, wondering what comes next. We are a mixed lot of odds and ends. There are several salespeople from the shops. A few cleaners. Several security guards. The early-morning shoppers who have ended up among the prisoners seem to be mostly women. There's one old and cranky-looking man. Everyone is keeping their heads down.

Except this old lady. She stands up and says, 'Excuse me!' all crisp and clear. The leader doesn't look around. 'I want to know what is going on. Who are you people?'

The leader continues to ignore her. But the old lady isn't the kind to take that lying down. 'I'm talking to you, young man,' she says.

The leader turns around and kicks her in the stomach. It's so unexpected and so brutal that several people scream. The old lady doubles over without saying a word. She grabs her stomach and stuff starts leaking through the buttons of her kurta. I can't see what it is, but it isn't blood. She lies on the ground, the breath knocked out of her, white in the face.

The leader reaches down and rips her kurta open. Packets begin to fall out. There is dal and rice and even a box of tea leaves. It is dal that is bleeding out of her. She is a shoplifter.

I think the terrorist will kill her. Instead, he starts laughing. 'So sorry to interrupt your shopping,' he says. 'Anyone else have any questions?'

Nobody says a word. The only sound is that of the old lady wheezing as she struggles to get her breath back.

Sitting right next to me is this little kid, about six years old. He's terrifically excited. 'Who are they, Ma? Why do they have guns? Are they the bad guys? Who are they going to shoot?'

His mother is struggling with the small toddler she holds in her arms. The toddler is shrieking and crying, and she can't get him to shut up. She keeps trying to get the older boy to be quiet and sit still, but he jumps up for a better look.

'What is it?' I ask. 'Don't let him cry. They won't like it.'

'My baby is hungry,' she says desperately.

The leader yells without even looking in our direction. 'Shut that child up or I will do it with a bullet.'

The mother tries to put her hand over the kid's mouth. He only screams louder and starts kicking. I take my dupatta and begin fanning him. The little boy whines and whimpers and slowly winds down into silence. We can all breathe again.

'Are the police going to come?' asks her older son. 'Are they all going to shoot each other? What's going to happen?'

'I don't know!' snaps the harassed mother. 'Nobody knows.'

Surely the police know what's going on by now. Surely somebody is doing something.

Kabir

I find myself sitting next to this fat boy. He's in the process of having a complete meltdown. He keeps muttering to himself. Then he turns to me and says, 'I can't die! If I die, my mother will clean my cupboard and find all the porn magazines I've hidden. I can't die.'

This is so unexpected that I start laughing. I just can't help it.

He is seriously upset, 'This is such a waste, dude! I've been on a diet for a month. If I knew I was going to die, I would have eaten everything. I would have really lived, you know what I mean?'

He doesn't need any encouragement from me to go on talking. 'I can't die, man! I've never had a girl. I don't even know if I'm gay or straight.'

I'm not ready to die either. And I'm just as badly off in the girl department. But I'm sure I'm straight. The only thing is, I don't have any major regrets. At least I didn't until this morning. Until I saw her.

Then, this little old lady stands up and begins asking questions. The leader wearing the black headband suddenly turns around and kicks her. All kinds of things start falling out of the old lady's clothes. Turns out she's a shoplifter. She picked a bad day to be stealing, I guess. We all sit there listening to her struggling to breathe. No one tries to help.

'That guy is really badass,' says the fat boy, terror in his voice.

'No,' I say. 'The really badass guy is that one.' I indicate the grey-haired man who had spoken quietly and politely to all of us. He radiates such authority that I have no doubt who the real power and the real badass in the group is. He is handling the whole operation without raising his voice once. Leaving the violence to the guy with the headband. As if he's above and beyond fighting, and belongs in a whole other zone of scary.

'That guy?' says the fat boy. 'What I can't understand is why he looks familiar.' I'm wondering the same thing.

The old man who had given his name as Mahendra Shyam Bhonsle gives a sudden snort. 'Young people. Ignorant! Don't you read? Don't you know anything? He was in the headlines yesterday.'

I haven't seen a newspaper in a month, but the fat boy has. 'It's that guy!' he exclaims. 'The one who planted the bombs in the trains. When so many people died.'

'Yesterday the court sentenced him to death,' says Mr Bhonsle. 'Today they were shifting him out to Yerawada jail. His name is Salim Mukhtar.'

Salim Mukhtar. *Shit.* If I had really managed to choose a God, I would have prayed. The bombs in the trains are only one of the long litany of things he's done, in a career marked with death and violence. He's evaded the police and stayed at the top of the Most Wanted list for over a decade. They had caught him by sheer accident. A regular raid that ended with the trapping of a very big fish. And they wasted no time delivering a death sentence via a fast-track court.

Salim is kneeling in a quiet corner, saying a quick prayer. When he finishes, he is handed a mobile phone. Every eye is on him. All the hostages seem to have figured out who he is. A little ripple of relief runs through the room as he goes into the next corridor. A private phone call. I wonder who he is calling.

The terrorists take up spots around the room. There seems to be nothing to do except wait.

I turn to the fat boy, who is now praying.

'So do you think we'll get a discount if we shop now?' I say.

He looks at me like I'm crazy. 'Did you just make a joke?!'

I nod. He is not amused. 'Seriously, man, some death-row crazy is going to shoot us in the head and you're making jokes.'

'I think I'd like to die laughing,' I say. He doesn't find that funny either. He edges away from me. That takes him closer to the old man muttering angrily to himself. Mr Bhonsle is a very angry old man.

Five minutes later, the boy leans towards me and whispers, 'I don't know what the old man's problem is, but he's seriously pissed off.'

'We're being held hostage by terrorists,' I say. 'I can understand him being pissed off.'

'Yeah, I know what you mean,' he says. 'I mean, I didn't even come in here to buy anything. I just wanted to look at some jeans. A few sizes smaller, you know, for when I came off my diet. Just looking. What were you doing?'

'Just looking,' I say. *Looking at the most beautiful girl that I have ever seen. Who just happens to be my best friend's girl.*

Mr Bhonsle joins the conversation in a burst of indignation. 'This is all wrong,' he says. 'I only came in here to buy a few envelopes. Today's the day I retire. I knew all the staff had got together to organize a lunch. They were going to give me a clock. They give everybody a clock.' He looks really upset. 'All I came in here for was some envelopes to put thank-you notes in. This is really irregular.'

I try to hide a grin. *Irregular.* I would call it a bloody disaster. The fat boy rolls his eyes. He looks at me and tries to smile. 'Hey, man, my name is Harish,' he says.

'My name is Kabir.'

'Yeah, yeah,' he says. 'We all heard. Is it really Kabir?'

'Yes,' I say.

'You were pretty brave.' Harish shrugs. 'I'm not brave. And I don't want to die.'

'I know,' I say. 'Those porn magazines.'

This time he really smiles. It's a small, scared smile, but it's a smile.

Salim comes back into the room. He looks at the group of frightened people huddled on the floor. Some are praying. Some are crying. He laughs. 'Do not be afraid. We will not harm you. You are our passports to get out of here.'

He seems exuberant. 'Everybody up,' he says. 'We are going to see ourselves on TV.'

Diya

We sit there on the floor for a long time, trying our best to be invisible. Some people are crying. There is a continuous soft murmur of people praying to their gods, pleading for help. The old lady has got her breath back and is sitting quietly in a corner. We are all waiting to know what's going to happen to us.

Then the leader comes back in and tells us to move.

We are all herded into the electronics department. Dozens of television screens are mounted from floor to ceiling. They are all tuned to the same thing: breaking news. Every channel is covering the terrorist attack on the police convoy that had been taking Salim Mukhtar to Yerawada. That's the name of the grey-haired man. I realize I know who he is. I listen with a sinking heart.

'An accident was engineered to block traffic while the rescue was carried out. Terrorists then ambushed the van that carried Mukhtar and managed to free him. However, they were unable to get away as a roadroller engaged in road work had been left parked, so that it blocked a side road.'

There is blurry footage from a mobile phone that shows a traffic jam and men with guns running between cars. There is the sound of gunfire. Then shots of a police van with the door gaping open. A roadroller sits squat in the middle of the road.

The presenter has a sombre expression as she says, 'The terrorists are now inside Luxore Mall. Police have cordoned off the area. It is currently unclear how many hostages are being held. There are unconfirmed reports of more casualties inside the mall.' The reportage switches to shots of the outside of the mall. Crowds are milling around. Police are struggling to control them. A policeman tries to make a statement while the press mobs and jostles him.

Salim watches it all, smiling. There he is, blown up in colour on every screen. The TV shows a gaunt, intense-looking man scowling at the camera. The image has little resemblance to the man who stands calmly beside us. The years have not been kind to Salim. He has spent the last three in a prison, waiting for a death sentence.

He turns the sound off. The presenter continues to mouth silently on the screens behind him as he turns to face us.

'As the lady told you—you are hostages. A good hostage is one who stays alive. I have more than enough to spare. So here are the rules.' He looked around at the numb people in front of him. 'There is only one rule. You will not be a hero. In real life, heroes die.'

No one can take their eyes off him. 'You will not try to escape. You will not try to do anything foolish. You will not move at all until you are told to. You will shut up. You will stay in one place. You will do what you are told.' He smiles. 'Only then you might stay alive.'

Nobody moves. Nobody says anything. Nobody tries to be a hero. 'We are going to make this easy for everyone,' Salim says. 'We have some demands. If the government meets them, you go free.'

A little murmur runs through the hostages. He makes it sound so simple. 'I know what you have been told. That we are dangerous, violent people. We are not. We are people with a wound. It pains us deeply, and no one will hear our pain. All we want is for them to listen to us.'

I guess it's simple irony that, at exactly that moment, the dozens of screens flash gory images of mangled bodies scattered among the wreckage of a train.

'We are not terrorists. We seek healing. We seek justice.'

Kabir

Freedom fighter. Seeker of justice. Men with guns in their hands seem to find an awful lot of fancy phrases to justify what they are going to do. Take away all the talk, and 'man with gun' equals 'killer'. But he obviously doesn't see it that way.

'Justice,' says Salim Mukhtar. 'That is all we ever demanded. Justice for the great injustices done to my people. Our place of worship was desecrated. It was destroyed.'

I can hear the sound of someone weeping quietly, trying hard to stifle their sobs. Salim's tone changes. He slips into the ranting voice that comes easily to those who whip up crowds or convince people to die for a cause. 'We asked for justice. Was it given to us?'

He walks up and down in front of the screens, searching for faces in the crowd in front of him. The facade of the quiet, polite man peels away. There is an intense glint in his eyes. Fervour in his voice.

'Every day, my brothers are harassed. Jailed. Accused. Killed in encounters. What do you do when you get no justice? You make your own. I decided to stand up. I made my own justice.'

Sure. What he really makes is bombs. What he did was stick a couple of bombs in a local train in Mumbai. Killed more than fifty people.

'They caught me, and I said to them—an eye for an eye. Is that not justice? IS THAT NOT JUSTICE?' He yells the last sentence, and the sound echoes in the large empty spaces of the mall.

As if anyone in our sorry bunch is going to stand up and argue with him. But no, it isn't justice. What had those people in the train ever done to him? They were just going home. Thinking about paying their rent. Worrying that their kid wasn't studying hard enough. Wondering if there was going to be water in their houses when they got back. Just ordinary people. Even his Muslim brothers were among the people killed in the train blasts. The same brothers he claimed to be standing up for. Terrorists are random killers. Period.

'They gave me a noose around my neck. To be hanged by the neck until dead.' He looks around at his captive audience. 'Well, I'm not dead yet. And I have my own idea of justice. All of you will learn what it is.'

I don't know if he is expecting applause. He gets a terrified silence.

He leans forward to look intensely at us. 'You be good hostages. I will pass a good sentence.'

Speech over, they count us. 'Thirty-six,' says one of the men. There are four of them, not counting Mr Death Sentence. Two more men come in, dragging a man in a security uniform. All that stands between us and the outside world are six terrorists and the man they have freed. Salim Mukhtar, the great Seeker of Justice, Bomb-maker, Killer of Random People.

The security man has been shot in the stomach and is covered in blood. They put him on the floor. He keeps moaning and moaning.

Everyone tries not to look at him. Except that old woman. 'Are we supposed to watch while this man bleeds to death?' she says.

'Sit down,' says the leader.

She doesn't. She gets up and walks over to the man.

'SIT DOWN,' says Salim, raising his gun.

'Young man, I am eighty-two years old. I've done enough living. I have no family. No money. My arthritis is agony. You can put a bullet in me anytime.' With that, she kneels down beside the injured man.

That old woman is the bravest person in the room.

Salim looks at her for a long moment. 'You remind me of my nani,' he says. 'She was an old hag like you.'

'I hope she's proud of you. Seeing you on television killing people.'

I think she's gone too far. But Salim starts laughing. 'You are exactly like her,' he says. 'I hated the old bitch.'

When the old lady touches the security man, he gives a gargled scream. Of all the ways to die, being shot in

29

the stomach is the worst. It's certain death, but it's slow, very slow.

There is nothing the old lady can really do for the security man. But she sits by his side and holds his hand and talks to him. And that is a lot.

Diya

I'm so tired. Being frightened all the time makes you very tired. All I want to do is lie down and go to sleep. But I don't dare. Beside me, the young mother, Malini, is struggling to manage both the toddler and the little boy. The toddler has fallen into a broken sleep. He keeps waking up and whining in a thin voice. The little boy keeps bombarding her with questions.

'When will we go home? Why are they keeping us here? Who are these men?'

I try to keep the boy occupied. His name is Manu. His mother is trying very hard not to burst into tears. She knows she shouldn't cry, or it will terrify the children.

'We are going to be out of here soon,' I say.

'How soon?' he wants to know.

'Just a few hours.'

31

'You're lying,' he announces. 'The man with the gun is going to kill us all. I don't mind dying. My dadaji died, and my mother said that he is now in a place where he gets everything that he ever wished for. I want a horse.'

'We are not going to die,' I say. 'The police are going to come and save us.'

'Will they have guns? I want a gun.'

Malini is very close to hysteria. 'I came in here to buy diapers,' she says. 'We had run out. We really need diapers. The children need to be fed.' Neither of us dares to ask for anything. We sit there on the floor, struggling to keep the children quiet. Hoping that Salim does not look our way.

Manu is fidgety and restless. He is fascinated by Salim's gun. Salim sits a little distance away, deep in thought, turning the gun over and over in his hands. He comes out of his reverie and looks up. When he notices Manu staring at his gun, he smiles and gestures at the boy to come over.

His mother notices too late. She tries to grab his arm, but he ducks and runs to Salim's side. She thrusts the toddler at me and scrambles to her feet, but another man with a gun steps between her and Salim. She sits down, trembling, watching with her hand over her mouth.

Salim takes the gun and puts it in the little boy's hand. 'Isn't she beautiful?'

The gun is heavy. Manu struggles to hold it.

Malini clutches my hand. She is shaking. 'Make Manu come back. Please, please,' she is whispering under her breath.

Salim strokes the gun. 'I call her "ammijaan". She gives me everything I want.'

'A gun can't be your mother,' says Manu. 'You need a real live mother.'

'Why?' asks Salim.

'To love you,' says the little boy.

'That's what they say,' says Salim. 'They teach you that your mother loves you. That every mother loves you. Mother earth. Mother India. But the truth is that mothers don't love their children equally.'

'My mother loves me!' says Manu.

Salim smiles a slow smile at the boy, then looks over at Malini. 'Really? Let us see.'

He gets to his feet and comes towards us. I'm still holding the toddler. Salim leans over and grabs him from my arms. Malini gives a despairing wail and tries to get her child back. Another terrorist fields her, laughing, and holds her back.

Salim walks back to where Manu is holding the gun. He takes it from the boy's hand and puts the gun to the toddler's head. He turns to where Malini is kneeling, breathless with terror.

'Go on, Mother. Choose. You can have only one child. This one. Or this one. Come on, choose. I'm going to kill one of them. Choose!'

He moves the gun from the head of one child to the other and back again, in a hypnotic dance that we all watch in silence. The toddler is shrieking in distress. Malini is frozen, staring from one child to the other. Then she stumbles forward and touches Salim's feet. 'Please!' she whispers. 'Don't make me choose. I beg of you.'

'Choose! NOW!'

Malini crouches there at his feet, unmoving. Then she gets up with a convulsive movement. She grabs the screaming toddler and holds him to her chest. Manu stares up at his weeping mother, betrayal on his face.

'See?' says Salim. 'We are all Mother India's children. But she loves some of them more than the others. To some of them she says, "This land is yours." To others she says, "Live within your *aukaad*. Put your head down." When she shares the roti, she doesn't break equal *tukda*s. And her children grow up and grow angry. They say, "We want our fair share."' He puts the gun in Manu's hand. 'When you don't get your fair share, you must take it.'

Manu stares at the gun and then looks at the man who had handed it to him. Salim smiles encouragingly. Struggling to hold the gun steady, Manu puts the barrel against Salim's stomach. A sudden stillness descends on everyone. Nobody dares to move. The terrorist nearest to Salim starts forward, but Salim shakes his head, stopping him.

Manu speaks into the silence, his voice trembling on the edge of tears. 'You are a bad man,' he says. 'You made my mother cry. You made her afraid!' His finger is on the trigger.

Salim does not move. He keeps talking in a calm voice. 'You're angry. Good. Now are you going to shoot me?'

Manu doesn't know what to do. He holds the gun there, his lower lip trembling, tears heavy in his eyes.

'Go on. Are you going to shoot me?' Salim's voice is gentle, coaxing.

The other terrorists are standing around, tensely watching the situation. Everyone's fingers are on their triggers.

Malini whispers, 'Don't. Please, Manu, don't. Look at me! Don't!'

Manu turns his head to look at his mother. She shakes her head, pleading with him with her eyes. Manu makes his own difficult choice. He drops the gun on the floor.

'Good boy.' Salim picks it up. He points the gun at Manu and pulls the trigger.

Malini's scream rocks us all. But the gun does not fire. Salim holds it out again. 'Safety catch,' he explains to Manu. 'You have to pull that down before the gun will fire. Understand?'

Manu nods, bewildered. Then Salim raises his hand and slaps him so hard across the face that the boy goes sprawling.

Malini reaches for her son. Salim turns to her and grabs her by the hair. He slaps her face repeatedly. Her head jerks back and blood spatters from her mouth. When he lets her go, she drops limply to the ground. Then he simply walks away.

In that moment, everyone sees him for what he is. I think we all realize that there is not much hope of us getting out of here alive. A deep silence of terror spreads across our little group.

Manu crawls over and puts his arms around his dazed mother. He tries to wipe the blood from her mouth. His little brother cries and cries.

How can people terrify little children? How can they look at another human being and pull the trigger? How can they kill and then carry on as if it is a perfectly normal thing? Humans. We are the most terrifying animals that walk the planet.

Kabir

Some freedom fighter. Terrorizing little children and their mothers. If everyone was scared before, now they are petrified. All waiting for the worst. But the worst is a very long time coming.

In movies, everything happens really fast. Eighty-four scenes, three action sequences, four songs, and it's all over in two hours. The hero beats up the bad guys, and everyone gets to go home smiling. In a movie, the hero would be on the roof by now, rappelling down to save us, bazooka on his shoulder. But real life isn't that way. And Salim was right. In real life, heroes end up dead.

We sit and sit, waiting for something to happen. Manu cries himself to sleep, clinging to his mother. The little kid falls into a fretful sleep. So does the angry old man, his head nodding and lolling about on his chest. The rest of us find it impossible to drop off, with every screen in front of us showing the hostage drama and blaring out updates. We follow our situation on the news across twelve different channels.

Two of the terrorists keep an eye on us. Salim comes and goes. He is on the phone a lot. I wonder who he's talking to, where the real power behind the acts of terror lies. Don't ever believe that acts of violence are random. Every act of terror is a move in a great game. The one that is played across borders by men who hold the fate of nations in their hands. They use fear to make us do what they want. We are just the stupid pawns. Hostages. And hostages are dispensable.

I've been watching the terrorists since I heard the first gunshots. Four of them know what they are doing. Two of them are extremely awkward. Just out of training. Holding the guns like they are too heavy. Holding them all the time. I know. I used to do it too. In time, you learn that a gun is damn heavy. You learn to keep it beside you at all times but try not to heft the weight around. It tires your arm and ruins your aim.

I look at our little crew of ragged morning shoppers. There is no way we are going to be heroes and take on the terrorists. Salim has given the right advice. Don't be a hero. Sit tight. Keep your head down. And hope like hell that someone is making plans to rescue you. I follow his advice. I wait quietly. Next to me, Harish begins to fall apart again.

'It's not fair. It's not fair that we die now. It is not our time.'

'Calm down, Harish.'

'I will not! I don't want to die.'

'Nobody does. Nobody. Not the man with a bullet through his gut. Not the soldier facing guns. Not even someone riddled with cancer and screaming in pain. No one wants to die.'

His eyes focus on me. 'I'm scared.'

'We all are. But are you going to let these shits see you scream and be terrified? Are you?'

'Swine. Bastards. No,' he says.

'Good,' I say. 'Calm down. Breathe.'

His chest heaves, but he struggles to get back in control. I slide down to sit beside him. We sit huddled knee to knee. It comforts us. I try to distract him.

'If this was an ordinary day, what would you be doing right now?'

'Playing with my dog. The poor bastard. The doctor said he has to go on a diet as well. He's just a mongrel I picked up off the road. But he's smart. I hide this ratty old toy, and he finds it. Every time.'

I keep an eye on Diya as he talks about his day. She just sits blankly in a corner. Not moving, not speaking. Her hair masking her face.

'He waits for me, you know. Sits at the door and waits until I get back from college. He'll just keep waiting . . .' He nearly starts to fall apart again.

'I don't know what's worse,' moans Harish. 'Waiting to be killed or being killed. It's killing me!'

I can't help laughing at his choice of words. He is very offended. 'You can laugh. You don't mind dying. You've got a death wish. Telling them you don't have a religion. You're mad, you know that?' He turns his back on me.

He is right. I wished for death because it's been such a long time since I've had something worth living for. And I've turned my back on what I'm told is worth dying for. But then I saw her, and I began to have the smallest of dreams again. A tiny flame. A little wish.

After about an hour of us sitting around, taking his advice, Salim comes back into the room. He seems to be charged. He claps his hands and says, 'Up! Everybody up!' We all get to our feet as quickly as we can.

Harish has fallen asleep. He lies sprawled in great slack-jawed sleep. I'm not surprised. Terror tires you out so much, you can sleep like the dead. He doesn't hear a thing. The rest of us get to our feet. He lies there, snoring. I shake him as hard as I can, but he doesn't move.

Salim stands looking down at him, greatly amused. 'Time to wake up,' he says. Then he fires his gun between Harish's legs. Harish convulses and wakes up, stunned and uncomprehending. I grab his arm and haul him to his feet. He is trembling.

They get us to stand together. I can feel Harish shaking beside me. Everyone is wondering what the hell is going to happen to us now.

'Smile,' says Salim. One of the men takes a photo of us on his phone. 'That's for the press. You guys are going to be the headlines.' He grins at us. 'You can sit down now.'

I've been watching Diya from the corner of my eye. At the exact moment that the photo is taken, she turns her head so her hair hides her face.

I can hear Harish behind me. He's crying, snivelling as softly as he can. He clutches my T-shirt urgently. 'Stay in

front of me, dude,' he says. 'Please don't let anyone see me.'
He has wet his pants.

We all sit down. I try to sit in front of Harish and cover as
much of him as I can. I'm so busy doing that, I don't realize
Diya has taken the opportunity to shift closer and sit next
to me. I only know it when the smell of lemons suddenly
washes over me. I turn my head—and there she is. I can't
stop staring.

'Oh man,' whispers Harish urgently. 'Please don't let her
see me.'

Diya holds my gaze as she asks, 'Earlier—before all this
happened—were you following me?'

'Yes,' I say. I can feel my heart thumping.

'Why?'

What can I say to her? 'Because you are beautiful.' It is
the truth. Well, at least half the truth.

She frowns.

'I'm sorry. I didn't mean to offend you.' She looks like
she is going to tell me off. Then her face softens.

'You tried to shield me. I'm not going to be offended.
Thank you.'

I can't think of a thing to say. She's sitting right there.
'Sure. Anytime.' Of all the stupid things to say! But my head
and my tongue short-circuit around her.

'Anytime?' she says. 'I wasn't planning on doing this too
often.' She smiles. I smile back. A girl who can smile when
the world is going crazy. My heart beats faster.

'What do you think is going to happen to us?' she asks.
Go on. Answer. Heart, calm down. Breath, come back.

'I like to say we're heading for a happy ending but I'm not that sure,' I say.

She indicates Salim, who is strutting around, talking on the phone. 'He scares me.'

'He's a dead man walking,' I say. 'He scares me too.'

The television sets are all still on, making a bank of talking heads behind Salim. Suddenly, something changes in the tone of the blaring voices—a ripple of different expressions and tense voices. The same news echoes from one screen to the other, carried on different lips in varying degrees of excitement.

'We have breaking news. The terrorists have just made their demands.'

Diya

I don't know why he risked himself to shield me. It was a kindness. Kindness always makes me afraid. It means you have to open yourself up to the other person. Give them something in return.

First, I thought he was one of my father's men. But he doesn't seem the type at all. Then I thought he was just some cheap roadside boy trying to harass a girl. He wasn't. I can't figure out who he really is. His clothes are crumpled and worn, and he smells stale, like he has slept in them. But he seems decent enough. He is too shy to meet my eyes, and his ears turn bright red when I thank him. When he steals looks at me, I find that his eyes are a startling grey. I'm about to ask him about himself, but then the announcement comes on.

'Just a few minutes ago we received a phone call and some photographs.'

Our photograph flashes on the screen. There we are. A bunch of terrified people staring into the camera. Faces that are stunned. Faces that are pleading. Faces that are blank with fear.

'The terrorists have demanded that a plane be put on standby with full fuel tanks. They have demanded safe passage to the plane and safe passage through Indian airspace. They said they have thirty-six hostages in their custody. They will release all safely on the completion of their demands.'

The cacophony of the announcement descends into speculation about where the plane will go. Experts analyse the kind of plane, the fuel load, the possible destination. Everyone agrees that the aviation demands have been made by someone who obviously knows what he is asking for. Then, the first politicians begin popping up on screen. Fingers are pointed at our neighbouring countries. Finger-wagging denunciations are made. There is talk of expelling ambassadors. Debates rage and pronouncements are made.

Midway through the news report, the angry old man gives a snort and stands up. 'You really think the government is going to do this? Fly you out free and safe from India? You are mad. And we are all dead people.'

Another woman screams at him, 'Why not? The government will give him a plane. They will!' Others join in to shout him down.

Mr Bhonsle spits out a single word, 'Fools!' Then he sits down again. People begin to cry louder. Some beg to be released.

They have the prime minister on and get his reaction. 'Our government will never give in to terrorist blackmail.'

They have the leader of the Opposition. 'Our government would never let innocent people die.'

They have a lawyer. 'The police have failed us. They have failed in their duty to protect innocent civilians.'

They have the head of an NGO. 'The judiciary has failed us. For every terrorist sentenced to death, another ten walk free.'

The chief of police. 'We are studying the situation.'

The home minister. 'We are studying the situation.'

Then a familiar face flashes on screen. Bhai Thakur. His voice is more strident than all the others. It rises out of the hubbub, loud and hypnotic. 'Only people of one religion are being held hostage. All of you who share the religion of those innocents who are being held, will you not rise up and take revenge?'

Bhai Thakur had started as a small-time goon, terrorizing an area full of slums. Then he learnt that religion could be a ticket to power. He claimed the position of saviour of the majority and became the power behind a string of violent riots, all aimed at minority communities. He is a big name in politics now. He's got there by whipping everyone into a frenzy about preserving Hindutva. Between rabble-rousing speeches and goons that bash anyone who protests, he has managed to get a foothold in the Hindu heartland. Today, he is wearing his trademark orange.

'Will we stand by and watch our brothers and sisters being slaughtered by those who would ruin our country?' He is warming up nicely. 'All you terrorists be warned—it is said in your holy book "an eye for an eye". We will take much more than an eye.'

This is too much for the old man. Mr Bhonsle stands up again and shouts at the screen. 'Shut up! We don't need this made worse by madmen like you!'

'He'll get us killed!' another woman shouts. A salesgirl is shrieking away. An expensively dressed woman begins screaming, 'Let me go! Let me go!' A frantic fear seems to seize everybody at the same time. The noise grows as panic spreads. The terrorists look uneasily at each other as the hostages scream and shout.

Salim ends it with a bullet. He shoots at a TV screen that has Bhai Thakur screaming his endless stream of hate. The screen explodes like a bomb going off. The hostages all instantly fall silent. Bhai Thakur continues to rant on the other screens. No one dares to listen.

Salim speaks softly and menacingly. 'You have all forgotten rule number one. Shut up and sit down!' Everyone fearfully subsides.

Salim says, 'Men like him make measures like this necessary.' Another terrorist spits on the ground. 'Do you think he would hesitate to cut thirty-six Muslim throats?' says Salim. 'But I am not him. I am still a reasonable man.'

Salim's tone is quiet, conversational. 'I have made reasonable demands. Now the government just has to be reasonable. A little plane so we can fly away—and all of you will be free.'

Not one word from the hostages. Even Mr Bhonsle is quiet. The only sound is the low moan of the security man who is dying very slowly.

The show is over. The armed men divide us into four groups, not willing to risk rebellion. I stick close to Diya and get shoved into her group. The other groups are moved to different sections of the store with a man each to guard them. They go quietly, all following rule number one. Salim goes with them.

We stay in the electronics section and watch TV.

It's me and Diya. Harish. The old man. Malini and her two kids. Two salesgirls. One of them slightly older. The younger one looks like an intern. They cling to each other. We've kind of all just hung together and have been placed in one group.

Mr Bhonsle mutters, 'That man was right. The government will never agree. We are dead people.'

'Will you *shut up*?' says Malini. 'The children are listening.'

Silence falls on us.

It is broken by a scream that goes on and on. The moaning of the gut-shot guard has become part of the background, like the non-stop chatter of the TV screens. Now he suddenly shrieks and convulses.

'Somebody please help me,' says the old lady. 'I need help!' Beside her, the man writhes and screams in a puddle of his own blood.

Kabir

All the men with guns are watching. No one is making any move to help. I feel ashamed for all of us. That old lady is worth more than all of us together. She turns away from the guards and looks at us. 'Please,' she says. 'Help.'

One by one, our little group turns away. Mr Bhonsle with a grunt. Malini with a helpless shrug. The two salesgirls drop their heads quickly. The old lady's eyes are sunk deep in wrinkles. They fix on me.

I get to my feet. A guard waves a gun at me. I get back down and crawl over to her.

Behind me I hear the rustle of someone else moving to help. It is Diya. The two of us bend over the guard.

The security guard is in another world. But even in that world, there is pain. His eyes have rolled back in his head and he is screaming. A thin, high-pitched scream that goes on and on.

We once had a dog when I was small. A little bitch that I befriended on the road. My mother agreed to keep her only if she was sterilized. When the effects of anaesthesia were wearing off after surgery, that dog howled and howled. She had no idea where she was. She just kept howling. The man is like that. He is very far gone. But he keeps screaming without stopping.

'I don't know what to do,' the old lady says. 'I just don't know what to do.'

I could have told her there's really nothing she could do. But the screaming moves me to action. I gently lift the cloth she has pressed into the hole in his stomach. Blood pulses out of it but the hole is small. I've seen enough of these to know that the problem is on the other side. The exit wound is normally massive.

Diya is trying hard not to look at all the blood. 'Come on,' I tell her. 'We have to turn him over.' She takes a deep breath and nods. Brave girl.

He is a heavy man and has gone absolutely limp. We struggle to turn him. Everyone watches. And he just keeps on screaming. We get him on his side and Diya gasps. The exit wound is huge. Like someone has taken a hammer and smashed him. Diya closes her eyes.

'No!' says the old lady. 'I didn't realize—'

'Give me cloth,' I say. 'Lots of it.'

Diya pulls off her dupatta and hands it to me. I wad it into the hole. It isn't enough. The old lady begins ripping strips off her kurta. I use them to try and keep the wad in place. But my hands are slick with blood and I can't tie the knots. They keep slipping loose. Diya leans over and holds the knot steady with trembling hands. Through all of it, the man screams.

She is so brave. So scared and so brave, determinedly helping me even as her hands tremble. Those beautiful hands. Covered with blood.

We put the man back down. The coppery smell of blood is in our nostrils. Diya's face is white.

I say to her, 'You did well.'

The old lady looks at me. I guess my face tells her what's going to happen. She stands up and shouts at the terrorists, 'This man needs a doctor! NOW!' Nobody moves.

'I said, this man needs a doctor! Can't you hear me?!'

One of the men pulls out a mobile phone and speaks into it. A few seconds later, Salim comes through the door.

'How many times do I have to say this?' he says. 'Shut up, sit down, and don't cause trouble.'

That old lady isn't shutting up. 'This man needs a proper doctor. Just let him go. You've got all of us. Just let him go.'

'What makes you think I care if he dies?'

'You have demands. You're negotiating. You have to give something to get something.'

'Not when you hold the gun,' says Salim.

'You think you're going to get out of here? You're in a mall. In the middle of the city. There are hundreds of policemen. You are going to die.'

'I have no problem with dying,' says Salim. 'I just want to take a whole lot with me when I go.' He turns and begins to walk away.

'Shoot him,' I say. Salim stops and looks at me.

'He's going to die anyway,' I say. 'Just spare him the agony.'

Salim stares at me for a long moment. Then he grins. 'I could have shot him a long time ago. I want him to suffer.' He starts walking away.

The old woman speaks. 'I hope that one day you beg for a bullet. Beg for it and no one gives it to you. I hope you struggle for every breath in agony.'

'*Allah Malik*,' says Salim and closes the door.

The old lady sits down slowly. She raises the man's head gently and places it in her lap. She strokes his hair. The screaming gradually stops. Her tears fall on his upturned face. I sit quietly on one side of her. Diya on the other side.

'I am glad that I'm going to die soon,' she says. 'The world can't break my heart any more.'

Diya

We sit there watching a man die. When I left the house this morning, all I wanted was one hour alone to think. I thought I had problems. Nothing compared to the problems I have now. Here I am, watching a man die and waiting for my own death.

The old lady wipes his face. 'I'm tired,' she says. 'I'm tired of this hate and anger. This has become such an angry world. So ready to kill.'

She looks at me and Kabir. 'You have to change things. You have to find a way to stop this. All this anger over religion. All this fighting.'

'We can't change anything,' I say. 'What can we do?' I hate it when old people turn to us and say it's up to us to change the world. They screwed it up. And we are supposed to clean up the mess?

My answer makes her really angry. 'If young people say they can do nothing, who is left?' She grabs my arm fiercely. 'You have to try. You must try and try and never give up. You can make the difference.'

I don't see how I can make any difference. But then Kabir speaks up.

'You must become the change you want to see in the world,' Kabir says softly.

'Yes,' she says. 'That's right. That is it exactly.'

She looks down at the dying man who has his head in her lap. 'That's what I tried to be. If I was lonely, I went out and talked to other people who looked lonely. If I was sad, I went out and tried to make someone happy.'

Her voice is soft. 'It has been so many years since I was loved. They all died. My husband. My children. All my relatives, one by one. But I just found new things to love. I have a cat. I feed seven dogs on the street.' She smiled at the memory. 'They really love me, those dogs.'

She sighs. 'I can't afford to feed them. Not on the little bit of money that I have. So I steal. I don't do it for myself. I don't mind going hungry. But I want to feed my dogs and cat.'

Kabir says, 'You're not a thief. And you're the bravest person I know.'

She smiles at him. 'Thank you.'

She takes my hand between her soft creased ones, and then Kabir's. She holds them tight. 'You must stay alive,' she says, 'and then you must make that life count.' There we are with our hands joined in hers. I avoid looking at him.

My life has never counted. I've always been just a pawn that my father used in all his grand plans. No one has ever asked me what I want. And I have never been able to change anything in my world. But that old woman makes me want to try.

'I will try,' I say.

'Yes,' says Kabir. 'I'll try.'

His hand is very warm. It makes me nervous. She lets our hands go and I pull mine back, trying not to make it look like I'm doing it too quickly.

'Is there anything else we can do for him?' she asks.

'No,' says Kabir.

'Then both of you go back and sit down. I don't want you to get in trouble. Just go.'

I put my arms around the old lady. 'I don't even know your name,' I say.

'Sharmila,' she says. 'Not that I ever was. My husband said I was badly named. He used to call me Jhansi ki Rani.'

Kabir kneels there, looking awkward. The old lady reaches out and pulls both of us into an embrace. She holds us close. We awkwardly bang shoulders, heads. We both pull back hurriedly when she lets us go.

As we crawl back to our places, the old woman is singing. A simple lullaby that a mother would sing to a child. Her voice cracks and wavers. But to me it is the sound of love.

Kabir

When that old lady hugs us, there is one moment when I'm so close to the girl that if I turn my head our lips will touch. I turn my face away, not even letting my mind go there. My heart, of course, thuds and skips.

All those nights that Aman had spoken of her, I had fallen asleep imagining a girl with sunshine in her hair. So many nights wondering if he saw her as she was or if it was just his love that coloured his gaze. Then I saw her. Now, I can't take my eyes off her.

I should have just mailed her the letter. Stayed as far away as I could. But Aman had taken that promise from me. And in the end, it's only that letter in my pocket that keeps me going night after night. It's taken me more than a month to get here. I should hand it over. Before I get shot and it stays with me forever, with her never knowing.

I touch the letter lying just over my heart. *Not yet. Not just yet.*

It's getting difficult to sit quietly. Everybody is tired, aching, dying to go to the toilet. The television sets blare on and on.

The demands seem to have caused a furore. Opinion is divided into two camps. There is the 'He's a terrorist and we can't give in to terror, or it will be worse' camp. And there is the 'Innocent people are being held—let's do whatever it takes to set them free' camp. Both sides yell at each other in television debates. And we wait. Our pictures are aired again and again. The picture in which Diya used her hair to cover her face.

Bhai Thakur is getting a lot of play on TV, mouthing off about how we've encouraged the minorities too much. How every Muslim is a terrorist. Each time he appears, all of us wince. The terrorists mutter and spit. Their anger makes the place tense. The bloody bigot is going to get us shot faster.

The channels have begun tracking down the hostage story. Mr Bhonsle turns out to have a wife who refuses to talk to reporters and shuts the door in their faces. She sounds just like him as she snaps, 'You people! No manners! Leave me my privacy!'

Other wives weep. Fathers beg for the return of their children. An old grandmother holds out her arms and wails, 'Take me! Take me, not my children! What will I have left to live for?'

Malini sits up suddenly and clutches her younger child to her chest. Her husband has appeared on the screen. He looks tired and almost ill with worry. Manu begins jumping up and down, shouting 'Papa!' He is an ordinary-looking man with spectacles and a shock of hair that falls across his face. He looks numb with fear. His spectacles keep slipping down his nose as he talks. 'Malini, I'm sorry. I should have said sorry in the morning. You have to come back. Please. I have to apologize. Come back to me.'

Malini's chest heaves and she begins to cry. 'We fought. There were no diapers, and he said he didn't have time to go and get them. He would have been here instead of me and the children.' Diya tries to comfort her, but she cries on and on, her shoulders shaking with silent sobs, so that she doesn't wake her sleeping son. Manu keeps asking when Papa will come and take them away.

Then, several phones start ringing together, their racket cutting through the voices from the television sets. It's the landlines on the desks.

Salim comes into the room and picks up a phone at the counter. 'I have been expecting your call,' he says. 'How are you, SP Sahib? The last time I saw you was in court.' He smiles. 'I asked for you especially. You put me behind bars. You can atone by helping me get away.'

The harassed father appears on one of the TV screens again, making an appeal to the terrorists to release his wife and children. Manu suddenly begins screaming for his father. 'PAPA! I WANT MY PAPA!' he shrieks. A petrified Malini tries to put her hand on his mouth to stop him. He begins to shake and thrash around.

'MAKE THAT CHILD SHUT UP!' shouts Salim.

We try. But he fights us and keeps yelling. Malini is shaking in fear. She slaps him. Holds him. Diya tries to hold on to him. But Manu does not stop. He is rigid and drumming his heels on the floor and screaming. We don't hear a word of the conversation that Salim is having. Then, suddenly, Manu goes limp and begins to sob bitter tears.

Even without the sideshow, I don't think Salim's conversation goes too well. He isn't smiling when he hangs up.

Diya

Salim hangs up and goes over to Malini. He leans down until his face is in hers and then shouts loudly. 'I thought I told you to keep that brat quiet!'

Malini is glassy-eyed, exhausted, holding Manu as he sobs, her other child clinging to her arm.

She suddenly seems to focus on Salim—and something snaps. 'You do it,' she says. 'YOU DO IT. You keep a child that is hungry and thirsty quiet!'

Salim's face changes with surprise. But she just keeps going, 'My children need food. They need water. We need diapers. We need to go to the toilet. We cannot go on sitting here like this. WE CANNOT!' She is having a complete meltdown. 'I will not sit here and listen to my sons crying FOR ONE SECOND MORE!'

Then she seems to realize what she is doing. Her hands go to her mouth and cover it. The fight goes out of her and the terror comes back. She scuttles backwards away from him, clutching both children close, looking horrified at what she has done.

Salim looks at her. Then he shrugs. 'Give them water. Arrange for them to go to the toilet. Escorted every time. The door stays open. You stay visible. Even the ladies.' The man with him nods. 'And get that kid some diapers. He's starting to stink.'

He walks away and Malini puts her cold hand in mine. She's breathing in short gasps, unable to believe what has just happened. She has screamed at Salim Mukhtar. And he hasn't killed her. We are getting food and water. Thank God.

Kabir

People have different things on their lists of stuff that makes them feel good. Sex tops a lot of lists. Massages. Showers.

But I tell you, there's nothing to beat a pee. Not when you've been holding it in for ages, and thinking that at any moment now you're going to let go and disgrace yourself. All that damn pressure builds up. In the head and lower down. And it gets to the point where you think that you're going to burst. And then you pee.

Best thing in the world.

I'm grinning idiotically. I keep grinning while washing my hands. Mr Bhonsle is at the next basin. He glares at me. 'What in this particular situation do you find so funny?' he asks.

'Nothing,' I say. I'm not going to explain.

'Youngsters of today!' he snaps. 'I don't know what they take seriously. In a life-and-death situation, they are laughing.' He turns to Harish, who has just stepped out of a stall and is also grinning.

'I stuck two rolls of toilet paper in my pants, and I have an empty bottle to pee in,' he says. 'I'm prepared!'

Mr Bhonsle glares at him. 'So you also find the situation funny, young man.'

'What?' says Harish.

'We are being held hostage by a madman, who has made impossible demands that are unlikely to be met. He is threatening to kill us all one by one if they are not. You find that funny?'

'But he's going to let us have food and water,' says Harish, trying to look on the bright side of things. 'That's kind of good.'

'Bah!' says Mr Bhonsle. 'Useless! Today's children. Useless!'

He storms out of the bathroom. The terrorist watching us indicates that we need to leave as well.

'What's his problem?' asks Harish.

I know what his problem is. I've seen the shaking hands, the frantic look in his eye. My brother has the same problem. It comes in the form of empty bottles that he throws every morning against the wall. Mr Bhonsle is an alcoholic. And he is being put through an unexpected and thorough detox.

We walk back to the electronics section. Harish keeps chattering about what we might get to eat. I'm not listening. I'm mapping the place. Checking out exits. Places to hide. It's training. An old habit. You never know when you might need a Plan B. I intend to have one.

Diya

We wash the children in the bathroom. Little Akku loves the water and splashes and gurgles. Manu turns the taps on and off, and runs around flushing every pot he can find.

It feels so good to wash my face and hands. Even Malini does her hair and begins to look like she's back in control, a bit.

'I can't believe you did that,' I say to her. 'You yelled back at a terrorist!'

She shudders. 'Don't remind me. I don't know what happened to me.'

'But you got us this. Thank you.'

Malini looks around, then slides over to me and whispers in my ear, 'I have my mobile. I was carrying two. I had one that needed to be repaired. I gave them that and slipped the second one into Akku's diaper.'

Shit. That could be a good thing. Or a very bad thing if she gets caught.

'What will you do with it?'

'Call their father,' she says.

'Don't,' I say. 'If he talks to the press, then it will be on TV.'

Her face falls. 'I need to talk to him. I can't let the fight we had in the morning be the last thing we said to each other.'

'No,' I beg. 'You'll just put yourself in danger. Put them in danger.'

'I can't carry on alone,' she says. 'I'm tired. I can't. It's been so difficult with two children. And he's never there. I can't carry on.'

I put my arms around her and hush her.

She lets out a strangled sob and says, 'I'm pregnant again! I didn't want to be but I am. I don't know what to do.'

'Don't think about it. You can't do a thing about that right now.'

'I haven't told my husband. I want to tell him. I need to talk to him. Please?'

'You can't call him,' I say. 'If they find the phone on you, you will be in trouble. Are you insane?!'

'What will I do with it?' she asks, suddenly frightened.

'Slip it to me,' I say. 'I'll hide it for you.'

She looks around to see if our guard is watching. He's looking the other way. She slips the phone into my hand. I go into a stall. I have to leave the door partially open. Then, I type a message as fast as I can.

'IT'S ME PAPA. I'M NOT IN COLLEGE. I'M IN THE LUXORE MALL. I WENT THERE TO SHOP. I'M ONE OF THE HOSTAGES. I'M SORRY.'

I wait for the reply. My heart is thumping hard. All of a sudden, I'm a frightened little girl again.

The phone vibrates in my hands almost immediately. 'DO NOT TELL THEM WHO YOU ARE. I WILL GET YOU OUT OF THERE.'

I sit there a moment. He will do something. He has power. He has people. And he won't lose me. Not with all the ambitions he has that are tied to me.

I place the phone in my bra and come out of the bathroom.

When we get back, one of the terrorists points at me. 'You,' he says. 'You know about diapers and things. Go get them. And the food.' He pushes a shopping cart towards me.

'I'll help.' It's Kabir. 'It'll take a lot of food and more than one cart to feed us all. I'll help.'

The man nods. Kabir takes the cart from me, and the two of us walk out of the door.

Kabir

I know this sounds crazy stupid, but I've never been to a mall before today. You can say my life hasn't been like that of a regular kid. No college. No hanging out. And definitely no malls.

My first time ever in a mall, and it's huge. It covers God knows how many thousand square feet. We step into the food section and it looks like one portion of a well-stocked heaven. There are rows running off in every direction. I stop at one row, and there are like a hundred shelves of just potato chips. Just chips!

It's crazy. Like some childhood fantasy come true. A huge kingdom of food in which you can wander and take what you like. The only problem is the man with the gun who is following us. But he gets a bit carried away with the food section as well. He gets himself a cart and begins pulling packets of stuff off the shelves.

Diya and I walk down the rows. I want to just walk like that for a while, beside her. Just to feel like we're out walking on an ordinary day.

'Let's pretend he's not here,' I whisper urgently to Diya. 'Let's pretend this is just an ordinary day. We just walked into the store. And we met. You couldn't reach something on the top shelf. And I helped you.'

She turns and looks at me. I think she'll tell me I'm crazy. Then a smile comes into her eyes and she shrugs. 'Thank you,' she says. 'I can never reach the top shelf.'

I grab the can without looking at what it is and toss it into the cart. 'So, you got a lot of things to buy? Long shopping list?'

'Mostly food. What are you looking for?'

'I don't know,' I say. 'I'm a browser. Not a list-maker.'

'Milk. Feeding bottles. Diapers,' she says firmly.

'Look at this,' I say, indicating the store, 'and all you can think of is the boring stuff? Let's go crazy! Let's just take everything we ever dreamed of.'

'When I was a kid, I used to be crazy for Nutties.'

I search the shelves and tip a whole shower of packets into the cart.

'What did you love?' she asks.

I grin sheepishly. 'I used to steal condensed milk.'

She pulls four cans off the shelf.

'Here's *aam ka panna*!'

'Here! Bourbon biscuits. Tutti frutti cake.'

'Peanut butter. Mango jam.'

We fill that cart with all the tastes of our childhood. All the food that made us happy.

'My music teacher used to give me Nutties. I hated *riyaz*, and he'd make me practise more by giving me two Nutties every five minutes.' She holds up a packet. 'That's twenty-five minutes of practice in there.'

'I would fight with my brother to get condensed milk tins to lick,' I say. 'Then we'd take them outside and find a stick and play cricket.'

'You like cricket,' she says.

'You like singing,' I say.

We look at each other and laugh. She takes a right turn with her cart. 'Come on, let's go do the boring stuff,' she says.

We pick up tea, milk, bottles of water, bread. Then she says, 'Look! They have a gourmet section.'

That turns out to be lots of fancy stuff that I've never seen before. She knows her way around it. She chooses five different kinds of cheese. And these little green things called olives.

'I don't know which chocolate to choose,' she says.

'I know,' I say, looking at the labels. 'Just take the most expensive.'

Then, on a shelf, I see a row of small tins. The label says 'Caviar'. I'm transfixed.

'What is that?' she asks.

'Caviar,' I say. 'Fish eggs. They're supposed to be very rare and expensive. Really fancy food.'

She wrinkles her nose. 'I'm vegetarian. You like fish eggs?'

'I've never eaten them,' I say. 'A friend of mine told me about them.' And with that, I think of Aman.

'What is it?' she asks, seeing that the moment has changed.

'Nothing,' I say hastily. 'Which is your favourite flavour of Maggi?'

I steer her back to talking, and the moment is gone. We go back to our little pretence. Talking just like two ordinary people meeting for the first time.

'Where are you from, Kabir?'

'Actually, I'm just visiting. I'm from Srinagar.'

'What are you doing in Mumbai?'

'Visiting a friend. He was in Kashmir, and we became good friends. This is where he used to live. You live here?'

'Yes. Live here. Study here. I'm in college.'

'So, what do you do besides studying? And singing?'

'Not much else,' she says. 'I don't go out much. I don't have too many friends. You?'

'Me neither. I mostly like being alone. It gives me space to think.'

'Me too.' We are both silent for a while as we search for the right kind of baby formula.

'What do you think about?' she asks.

'Life. How strange it is. People. Right and wrong.'

'Me too,' she says. 'I think about how cruel people are. There is nothing so bad that one man will not do it to another.'

'Not all men are like that. I think sometimes of the sudden kindness of strangers.' Aman. My kindest and only friend. How many kindnesses he has given me.

'I think of being alone,' she says. 'I am not brave enough to be alone forever.' Sadness drifts into her eyes.

Before I can ask a question, she quickly says, 'Let's go get some ice cream. I love ice cream.'

The frozen food section blows me away. The freezers are rooms you can walk into. And there is a whole room full of ice cream. An entire room! Every colour and flavour you can imagine, and dozens that you've never ever thought of. I walk along the shelves, calling out the flavours in astonishment. 'Banana caramel. Butter pecan hazelnut. Cheesecake. Coffee almond. Mint chocolate chip. Peanut butter. Green tea. Green tea?!'

She laughs at my astonishment. 'You've not had too much ice cream?'

'In Kashmir there are only a few months of the year when you can.' I say. 'The rest of the time it's too cold.' As the cold breath of the freezer wafts over to me, I'm suddenly gripped with homesickness.

'If you could be any place other than here right now, where would you choose?' I ask her.

'Me? The beach. Definitely the beach. Somewhere with white sand and clear blue water, where you just look down and you can see the fish. And you?'

'In a forest in winter. The snow makes everything so quiet. You can hear every breath of yours, and you start noticing how alive you are. That the trees are beautiful. That way up in the sky there are three birds just sailing around in lazy circles enjoying the winter sun.'

She tilts her head and watches me. 'You love Kashmir very much.'

'Yes,' I say. 'An emperor once said, "If there is a paradise on earth, it is here, it is here."'

'I wish I could see it,' she says.

'Maybe one day you will.'

She shakes her head. 'I don't know if we are going to get out of here alive.' Our little world of pretending is broken in that moment, and we are back being hostages with a guard watching over us.

We step out of the freezer and find ourselves facing rows and rows of fancy bottles. It is the wine section. I pick up a bottle, but the guard with us shakes his head and waves his gun in warning. I put it down.

We walk over to frozen foods to find chapattis and ready-made meals. Her sadness is back. I want so much to take it away.

'What makes you happy?' I ask her.

'Singing,' she says. 'And you?'

'I can't sing. But I love old Hindi songs.' I gently ask, 'What makes you sad?'

'Being away from people I love,' she says, after a brief hesitation. 'Losing them. Waiting and waiting to see them again.'

'I know that feeling,' I say. 'I lost a brother I loved very much.'

'Lost him?' she asks.

'Yes,' I say. 'I don't want to explain.'

'Then don't,' she says. 'People don't understand real grief. They think we are too young to know what real sadness is. Or real love.'

'But we aren't,' I say. 'Age has nothing to do with how deeply you can feel.'

'No,' she says.

I lost a brother. I lost two of them. Both in one day under a fine blue sky bright with sunshine. I don't want to go on without them, but I have a promise to keep.

I wonder how to make her sadness go away. I spot a small bakery shop in one corner of the food section. 'Look!' I say. 'Let's get Manu an un-birthday cake. They've even got candles.'

That brings a smile to her face. The bakery has a little corner with everything you need for a party. We go all the way and add paper hats, balloons, some crayons and a drawing book.

'Let's take the microwave,' she says.

I unplug the microwave from behind the counter and shove it in our cart. It would be nice to have hot food.

The diapers section is right next to the personal hygiene section. While she reads the packets and struggles to understand what size to buy, I furtively take a couple of bottles off the shelves. Deodorant. And mouthwash. I just don't want to breathe acid on her while we talk.

I wonder whether I should take toothbrushes for everybody, just in case we are here tomorrow morning. But I think that might make them more demoralized, so I don't.

Then I nearly blow it. We take a final round to see if we have missed anything, and I quietly take something off a shelf. Then I ask her, 'If you could have one thing right now, any one thing, what would you ask for?'

'Bubblegum. I love it. I've finished every single piece I had with me. I couldn't find it on the shelves.'

I hand her a packet of bubblegum. She freezes. 'How did you know that?'

Her eyes are on me. Frightened and puzzled and worried. I have to think really quickly. 'I just picked up some for myself. Breath freshener, you see.'

Her eyes stay on me, wary. So wary.

'You like it too?' I say. 'That's great. We have one thing in common.' To my relief, she takes the packet. Phew.

I check whether we have enough stuff, quietly kicking myself for being so obvious.

'Haven't you finished?' asks the terrorist. His cart is piled high.

'Yes,' I say, turning to her. 'Gotta go. I have some people just dying to see me again.'

She smiles. 'Me too. Nice meeting you like this.'

'Me too. I think we could be friends,' I say. 'I don't have too many.'

'All right,' she says.

I wave at her and she waves back. Then we walk back with our loot.

We've come back with not one cart, but three. All filled to the brim with the finest. The sight of all the food seems to fill Harish with new energy. He puts himself in charge of handing it out, plugging in the microwave with great enthusiasm and ripping open packets.

'Did you know,' he says, handing out the goodies, 'any man condemned to die is allowed a final fantastic meal?'

'I wonder what Salim chose,' I say. 'He was supposed to be hanged tomorrow.'

Harish isn't listening. 'Look! You got pizza. And olives. Caviar? I don't know what the hell that is.'

'It's fish eggs,' I say. 'Russians love them.'

'Damn. I'm vegetarian.' He holds up slabs of chocolate. 'Oh! I love you both. You got chocolate! And ice cream!'

I've chosen butterscotch and mango cream. Harish almost kisses me. The two terrorists watching us wander over to check what the excitement is about. They take the mango cream.

Harish heats everything in the microwave. He serves it on paper plates.

We are all starving by then with the smells that fill the room, but first we cut the un-birthday cake. Manu's face when he sees all the balloons and party hats is a sight. There is no question of lighting the candles, so we just pretend. He blows at the candles and we clap. He is so excited, it makes all of us happy. His little brother gurgles and laughs and chases the balloon that I blow up for him. For the first time, a few smiles show on the faces of the terrorists. We cut the cake and give them some. They give us back some of the mango cream. Harish seems to forget that they are terrorists. He hands them more cake. He urges everyone to eat more. He hands out cold drinks. He behaves like the generous host at a good party. I think all of us, the terrorists included, are playing pretend while the meal lasts.

The only two who stay out of the make-believe of normality are Sharmila and Mr Bhonsle. The old lady takes the water we give her, but refuses to eat. She sits there patiently, crooning to the guard.

Mr Bhonsle takes the food, but sits there glaring at the world. I sit next to him, and he snorts at me. 'What? You think this is a time to have parties?' I slide out the present I've got him from under my shirt. I managed to grab a small bottle from the rack of wine as we went past. He stares at it, then quickly hides it behind him. I get a reluctant nod as a thank-you.

Behind us, the television screens continue to flash their never-ending story. We ignore them for just a little while.

Harish comes up to me. 'Introduce me to the girl,' he says.

'Why?' I ask.

'What a stupid question!' he says. 'She's beautiful.'

'I thought you were getting ready to die,' I say.

'I'm still alive,' he says. 'Not dead yet.'

So, I introduce them. 'This is my friend, Harish. He wanted to meet you.'

'You can call me Harry H.'

'What?'

'That's my stage name. I'm going to be a deejay. Soon.'

That guy is so full of shit. From being terrified to chatting up a girl. Crazy what a full stomach can do to people. I think everyone there is pretending that this is going to have a happy ending. That they are all right and everything is going to be fine. But I've done my own share of pretending. Who am I to judge them?

Diya

We all sit down to eat together. It feels like a picnic. Kabir's friend Harish is really funny. 'So, you shop here often?' he says.

'Not any more,' I say. 'I'm planning to give my loyalty card back.'

'Maybe they have hostage situation bonus points. For every hour you get a zillion.'

Harish eats like this is his last meal. I understand why. In between hasty bites, he tries to find out everything he can about me.

'So, are you an only child?'

'Yes,' I say.

'Which college?' I tell him. Kabir stays silent through our conversation.

'Hey, I saw you at the last festival,' he says. 'That's why you looked familiar. You were singing!'

'Yes,' I say.

'Hey, you were good!' he says. 'You were great. You could have a whole career. Win *Indian Idol*, you were that good. You came out there and you rocked it!'

I don't reply. I can't say a word without crying. His words have suddenly brought back that night in vivid detail. The crowd in front of us throbbing with noise. Me, so nervous that the mike was vibrating in my hand. Then a sudden touch on my shoulder. I knew that touch. It steadied me. Gave me courage. Made me suddenly feel like I was breathing in air and breathing out light.

Aman.

'Hey,' says Harish. 'What is it? What did I say?'

Kabir

Bastard. He's stealing my jokes. Chatting up the girl. Even managing to make her smile. Then he talks about her singing and suddenly she is sad. Harish tries very hard to get her back into the conversation, but she is far away, lost in some memories that make her keep blinking back tears. She uses her hair as a curtain to hide her face. That beautiful hair. I want to reach out and run my fingers gently through it.

Harish tries his desperate best, but it is only when we hit the chocolate that Diya begins to talk again.

'What I can't understand is why nobody is doing anything,' says Harish. 'I mean, where is the army? Where are the Black Cat commandos?'

'Guarding some doddering old politician,' I say.

'Man, someone has to do something!' he says.

'They should have done it a long time ago,' I say. 'If you let injustice lie until people are willing to pick up guns to get what they want, then you've let it lie too long.'

'Injustice? They're terrorists, man!'

'But they have a point. Their temple was pulled down.'

Harish is furious. 'But they blew up things in retaliation, didn't they? Bomb blasts across Mumbai. In trains.'

'And in other places, riots happened in which the police stood by doing nothing. Mobs went in search of Muslims with lists in their hands.'

'They blew up the twin towers, man!'

'Stop it, you two!' says Diya suddenly, furious. 'Stop it. If you try to figure out who started it you'll have to go back to the beginning of time. One injustice does not justify another. Everyone has done unjust things to each other. Everyone has killed. There is nothing you can do about the past. You can only decide what you are going to do about it today.'

Harish and I are silent. She is so angry, but she makes so much sense.

'What can we do about it, man?' says Harish. 'It's all political.'

'Yes,' says Diya. 'A lot of it is political. A lot of it is manipulation and manufactured. Yes, politicians and religious leaders use it all.' Her voice turned to contempt. 'But we let it happen. It's people like us who believe things without checking the facts. Who turn a blind eye when bad things happen. Who don't stand up and say—this is wrong!'

'Come on. We can't change anything,' says Harish.

Diya speaks softly, but her voice is filled with feeling. 'I used to think like that. Until Sharmila made me promise.' Her eyes go the old lady bent over the dying man.

'I've been thinking about what I can do. And I think there are many times when you can stand up and say—this is wrong. That's where it starts from. From ordinary people who are sick of all the hate taking a simple stand. Writing to newspapers. Stopping someone from saying ugly things. Just saying to someone, "No, that is wrong". I think that's where we start from. From us. From each one of us.'

She suddenly realizes she has the attention of the whole group. Everyone has stopped eating and is staring at her. She shrugs and quickly looks down, letting her hair fall across her face. She uses that hair like a curtain. To shut herself off from the world.

Diya

Dinner over, I keep Manu quiet by making him draw. We settle down with paper and crayons, and Kabir joins us. I slide a piece of paper and some crayons over to him. He fiddles a bit, but then begins scribbling away on his piece of paper just as enthusiastically as Manu. But while Manu draws men with guns, Kabir draws a forest, deep in snow, with a little space in the middle.

'What's that?' Manu wants to know.

'It's a house in a forest,' says Kabir.

Manu turns out to be an art critic. 'That's not a house,' he says. 'It's just a square in the middle of a white field.'

'It is a house,' Kabir insists.

'It's got no roof.'

'That's so that you can see the stars.'

'It's got no windows.'

'That's so that the wind can come in.'

'It's got no door.'

'So nobody needs to knock. Everyone is welcome. Always.'

I think about that. A house far away in the whiteness of snow. Where there is a roof of stars and where everyone is welcome. I would like that.

Manu looks at Kabir's artwork again. 'I like it. What is your house called?'

'I call it a House of Stars,' he says, signing it.

'I'd like to live in a house like that,' I say.

Kabir smiles and hands me the drawing. He has signed it 'Afzal'.

Kabir

As far as good moments go in a really lousy situation, this is perfect. She smiling at me. Me smiling back. Then Mr Bhonsle screws it up.

He gets to his feet with a great snort. He is swaying.

'This should not be happening,' he announces loudly. 'This should not be happening in a democracy.'

If he was mad earlier, now he is just furious. I shouldn't have given that old man his bottle. He's dead drunk.

He puts the bottle down with a bang. 'I only came in here for some thank-you cards,' he says. 'Why should I be a hostage? This has nothing to do with me.'

'Sit down,' I tell the old man. 'You'll screw it up for all of us.'

'Thank-you cards,' he says. 'I was supposed to retire today. I didn't want to retire. They asked me to. Told me it was time.'

Harish tries to hush him. The old man just gets louder and more angry. 'And then they bought me a clock. The perfect gift. It's time. You're old and useless. It's time!'

The old man staggers forward a few steps. We try to hold him back but he's surprisingly strong, pushing away our hands. He shouts. Years of talking over the chatter of bored students have given him a voice of great power. A schoolteacher's voice.

'They got rid of me. And what did I do? I bought a bunch of envelopes to put thank-you cards in.'

He reaches into his pocket and pulls out a bunch of small envelopes. He flings them into the air. They rain down on us like confetti. He stands there in the rain of envelopes and laughs.

'Thank you, Mr Bhonsle. Thank you for giving your whole life to teaching bored students who didn't care. Thank you for holding the best attendance record among the teachers. Thank you for standing up in front of the class and hearing them all giggle at the last desk.'

'Enough, teacher,' says one of the two terrorists guarding us. 'Shut up and sit down.' They are watching him with amusement. I guess a full stomach has made them feel better as well.

'I will not shut up!' says Mr Bhonsle, incensed. 'I have the right to speak. Article 19 of the Constitution gives it to me as a Fundamental Right. I will not shut up.' He points at the terrorists. 'And you—you are illegal. There is no place for you in our Constitution. India is a secular republic. Secular! Do you even know what that means? No difference between one religion and another. You are illegal and the law shall deal with you.'

'They have to catch us first,' says one of the men, grinning.

'We have the finest laws in the world. Do you know that? The very finest Constitution. But we are a nation of lawless people. A nation that has no civic sense. A nation where any man who has a gun thinks he can get away with anything.'

No prizes for guessing that the old man teaches political science. He wags a finger at us. 'Laws are only as good as the people appointed to enforce them. What's the point of having the world's best laws if we have the world's most corrupt guardians?'

'But you know what the real problem is?' he continues, standing there swaying from side to side. 'The problem is not that our lawmakers are corrupt. The problem is not that the police are corrupt. The problem is not that our administrators are corrupt. The problem is that we are corrupt.' His shaking hand points at us, one by one.

'You want something done? You look for a person of influence. You want something done fast, you pay.'

He laughs. 'Oh, we complain about the state of things. Then we look for the shortest, easiest way to get things done—and damn the law.'

The terrorists are still smiling and enjoying the show. 'Masterji, the bell has rung. Sit down,' says one of them. He comes over and points his gun at Mr Bhonsle, smiling all the while.

Mr Bhonsle seems to suddenly run out of indignation. 'And so, class, let me end the lesson by saying, there is no hope for this nation. You and I are what is wrong with it. Jai

Hind!' He sits down abruptly. So abruptly that his feet give way and he sprawls on the ground. Then he just turns over and falls asleep.

I lie there thinking about what he has said. I think about the promise I made to Sharmila to try and change the world. This is a crap world to try and change. The old people have screwed it up well and good.

As if to emphasize how screwed up the world is, the image of Bhai Thakur flashes on screen. He is addressing a massive rally. 'Will we let someone hold a gun to the head of Mother India? To take her hostage? Bharat Mata is in danger. It is time for us to rise.'

I don't know what makes him think Bharat Mata belongs exclusively to him and his gang. Hindus aren't the only ones who belong here. We've got Christians, Sikhs, Jains, Buddhists, Muslims—a whole rainbow of religions. All of whom are born and who live on this soil. What does our religion have to do with the love we have for the place we call home? We love the land we are born on. Rabble-rousing idiot. He is a terrorist in his own way.

I turn to look at Diya. She's staring at the screen with a peculiar expression. I think it's hatred. Then she drops her head and her hair hides her face.

The letter is still in my pocket. I can feel it heavy against my heart. *Give it to her. Get it over with.* I hesitate. Against all odds, I have grabbed a few moments with her and it has made me greedy. I want just a few more. Just a little more time before it runs out for both of us.

Harish eases his weight down beside me. 'I am so never going on a diet again. Food is so like God. It is God!'

'You've been blessed pretty heavily by God in that case,' I say.

'I've got three slabs of chocolate in my pocket. I want to eat them, but I know I'm going to be sick. But I definitely want to eat them soon. I don't want to die thinking there was chocolate in my pocket and I never ate it. I don't want to die with regrets.'

I laugh. Harish opens a button on his pants to accommodate his bulging stomach and says, 'So, do you have any regrets?'

'Like what?'

'I don't know. Stuff that you thought you'd do. But which you won't now. Like getting married, having kids and stuff.'

'I never thought I would live long enough to get married and have kids and stuff.'

'You are seriously weird, dude,' says Harish. 'How long have you been walking around with a death wish?'

I shrug. He is silent for a while, then he speaks again. 'Falling in love. I'd like to know what that is all about.'

I say nothing.

'I mean, how do you know that you're in love? Right now, any girl sits next to me, my heart starts beating faster. You should have heard it during dinner when Diya was sitting with us. I thought I was going to have a heart attack and die.'

'I thought you were going to have a heart attack too, from how much you were eating.'

'I mean,' says Harish, 'I could be in love with Diya. But is it her, or just any girl? So how do you know a girl is really the one?'

'You know,' I say. 'You just know.'

'And then what? You're happy! You're in heaven. You're willing to die for her!' His expression becomes worried. 'What if she's not into you, dude? What if she can't stand you?'

'That doesn't stop you from loving her. Love comes. And all you can do is accept it.'

'But dude—it must hurt.'

'Better to have loved and hurt than not know what it is at all.' My eyes are on her as I speak.

Harish looks at me. Then at her. Comprehension dawns on his face. 'It's her. You're in love with her!'

I look away and shrug like it isn't true. But Harish is all over me. 'Lucky bastard! What are the odds of that? You meet when your lives are in danger. And you find love!'

'At least keep your damn voice down!' I hiss.

He looks at me seriously. 'You know we might die, right? This might not be the best time to fall in love.'

'What better time could there be?' I say. 'At least I know what it's like before I die.'

'Bastard,' he says. He looks across to where Diya is sitting. 'She tries to hide it, but she just looks sad all the time.'

For a guy who nearly got shot for not paying attention, he does pay quite a bit of attention.

After that conversation, he is impossible. He keeps darting looks between Diya and me. He stays glued to any conversation at all that we have. If she says, 'pass the water', Harish shoots upright and watches us avidly.

I can't give her the letter with him watching my every move.

Idiot.

Diya

Manu won't go to sleep. He insists that I tell him a bedtime story. 'But I don't want one with a hero in it,' he says.

'Why not?'

'Because it's all lies. No hero comes to save you. Not Salman. Not Shahrukh, not Maharana Pratap, not Chhota Bheem, not anyone!'

'How do you know?' I say. 'We're just at the wrong part of our story. We're at the part that is all scary, and it looks like the bad guys are winning and no one is going to help. But the story isn't over yet. Picture *abhi baaki hai*, yaar.'

'Do you think someone will come?'

'Of course,' I say, lying.

'You think it will be my papa?'

'I bet right this minute your papa is making a really great plan to save you. He is with the police, and they are thinking up a really good plan.'

'When will he come?'

'Close your eyes and go to sleep. When you open them, he might be here.'

He finally closes his eyes and is fast asleep in a minute.

Kabir is watching me. He watches me a lot. I wish he would stop. It makes me uncomfortable. It feels like he can see things that I don't want people to see with those grey eyes of his. He's a strange boy. I can't understand him. I only know that he kind of makes me feel safe.

Kabir speaks quietly, trying not to wake Manu. 'What are you going to tell him when he wakes up and there's no sign of his dad?'

'He needs something to believe in. We all do.'

Kabir shrugs. 'There are no rescues coming.' There is bitterness in his voice. 'There are no heroes. There never have been. You just think there are, until you get to know people a little bit better.'

I don't even know if I want to be rescued any more. It's so peaceful to be just stuck here in this time. Not to have to think about tomorrow, or the rest of your life and wonder whether you would get married, be happy, be content. Tomorrow might just not exist. It's terrifying, but also kind of freeing.

'We should rest,' I say.

'I can't sleep,' he says. 'You want to talk for a while?'

'Yes,' I say.

'What would you like to talk about?'

'About you. I think you should tell me who you really are,' I say softly.

Kabir freezes. He just sits there, not moving. I watch his eyes to see if he is lying. 'You keep watching me. You knew I liked bubblegum. Who told you that? Who are you?'

'Nobody,' he says. 'A perfect stranger.'

'You flung yourself over me to protect me. A perfect stranger doesn't do that. Who are you?'

'Nobody at all,' he insists. 'Just an ordinary everyday guy stuck in a crazy place. Who likes bubblegum.'

I don't believe him. 'Did my father send you? Are you one of his men? Have you been told to keep an eye on me? Report back to him?'

'No,' he says. 'I don't even know who your father is. Who is he?'

He can't be my father's man. Not with the name he accidentally signed on the paper. I don't answer his question. Instead, I ask him another one.

'Who are you, Afzal?'

I can see the shock on his face when he hears this. He doesn't try to deny it. 'How do you know my name?'

I hand him the drawing that he had signed and given me. 'Is that your name?'

'Yes,' he says. 'Damn. I didn't realize I did that.'

'Is that the truth? Are you telling me the truth?'

He looks up at me and holds my gaze. 'I swear that is my name. I swear I am from Srinagar. I swear your father didn't send me.'

I ask him again, 'Who are you?'

'I'm an idiot,' he says. 'I saw you from across the road. Followed you in. Then I changed my name so I could stay.'

I really wish I could believe him.

'Why did you follow me?'

He says nothing but he does not meet my eyes.

'Why do you try to protect me?'

The question seems to make him very angry. 'Because I'm an idiot! I saw you from across the road and—'

'Stop!' I tell him. I don't want to know. I don't want to see what's in his eyes as he looks at me. It's wrong. All wrong.

I take a deep breath and tell him my secret. 'There is someone I love very much,' I say. 'I'm waiting for him. You really shouldn't hope for anything at all.'

He doesn't look at me. 'I'm not hoping for anything at all,' he says. 'I'm not hoping. I quit on hoping some time ago.' He makes it sound so sad. I harden my heart. I don't want to sympathize with him. I have nothing to give him. Not even kindness.

'Did you ever want something impossible?' he asks. 'I mean, you knew it was impossible, you weren't hoping, but just for a little while in your head you were pretending it could be real.'

I want to tell him to stop. But I have pretended. I know how it feels.

'Please,' I say. 'It's no use.'

'I know,' he says, 'but fate has brought me here at this time to be with you. Let me just be here until . . . until whatever is meant to happen, happens.'

'You mean until we die.'

He looks me in the eye. 'We're in the middle of craziness. We're out of control. We don't know what's going to happen. I just want to be there.'

'I'm afraid of dying alone,' I whisper.

'You won't have to. Maybe that is what fate put me here for. Just to be there for you.'

'It shouldn't have been you.' I put my hands over my face and begin to cry. It shouldn't have been him. It should have been Aman.

I weep and weep. He makes no move to touch me. Just sits there while I cry. I cry like I have cried night after night for Aman. I cry until the tears run out. Except that they never really do.

'I think I'll try to go to sleep,' I say.

'You sleep,' he says. 'I'll keep watch.'

I curl up on the floor and close my eyes. I know if I open them, I'll see him sitting there, watching me. It no longer makes me awkward. I have a friend I can die with.

Kabir

What a stupid thing to do. I hadn't even realized I had done it. Signed my real name. And then she confronted me. It was the right time. I should have told her everything. Given her the letter. Finished it. But I held on. So little time. So little time. I couldn't open my hand and let fall these few moments I held so tight. *I am sorry, Amanbhai. I will give her the letter when she wakes up. These are the last moments that I will steal.*

I watch her sleep. She turns away from me, curled into herself, everyone shut out. But I am happy just to watch her. I have no other expectations.

Around us, others are dozing. The two shop girls are whispering, consoling each other. The television sets drone on, anchors replacing each other in a frenzied relay. The shots show a crowd of people outside the mall. Dozens of cameras and the flat circles of mobile satellite stations. Policemen have set up a cordon. Everyone is waiting. The demands have been made. Something has to be given.

Even the terrorists are dozing. But I'm awake and alert.

Suddenly, there is noise. Salim screaming at us. 'Get up! GET UP RIGHT NOW!'

The other hostages are being shoved into the room. They too look disoriented and petrified. One woman is crying hysterically. Two other women are trying to hold her as she thrashes from side to side, weeping. They crowd in, worried and afraid.

'Get up right now!' yells Salim. He stands in front of the screens. 'I want you to watch this. I want you to pay attention.' No one moves their eyes from him.

'I am a man who has tried to be just and fair. I gave your government an offer. And they took me for a fool. We've been waiting five hours now. I have run out of patience.'

He gestures. Two of his men step forward, and as the crowd shrinks back, they grab a random man. His wife begins to scream. He fights them, but one of them clubs a gun across his face and he is dragged, dazed and stumbling, from the room.

'Watch,' says Salim. 'And learn.'

Everyone turns with dread to the screens. All of them show a single image while the presenters' voices speak in a multitude of tones. 'Salim Mukhtar has just sent an ultimatum.'

We scarcely hear what the presenters are saying. Everyone is riveted to the images on the screen. We see the entrance to the mall. It is deserted. The police have set up a cordon at some distance. The door opens and the man who has been dragged from our midst stumbles out. He stands there blinking in the sunlight, looking bewildered. He has no idea what to do. He takes a step forward and suddenly falls to the ground. He has been shot.

In a bizarre echo, we hear the actual shot before it sounds from the screens.

The screaming woman begins to shriek louder. 'They've killed him! They've killed him!'

It isn't over. The man isn't dead. As we watch in horror, he begins to move. Slowly, he gets to his knees and tries to crawl down the stairs. He is heading for the cordon.

A volley of shots rings out. We hear them reverberate from outside and from the screens. We see him jerk again and again. Somehow, he just doesn't go down. He gets to the first step. He slowly begins to crawl down the steps, leaving a wide streak of blood behind him. He moves very slowly. The shots have stopped. Nothing seems to be happening except that man keeps moving with incredible slowness, fumbling his way from one step to another. Second step. Third. Fourth.

Then the door opens. A terrorist runs out, takes aim and puts a bullet through his head. He runs back through the door. The man slides down another step or two. No one moves as they will him to get up. To make it to the safety line of cameras and policemen. But this time he is still.

Salim steps in front of the screens to face us. 'I have given the government a new deadline. One hour. One life. Every hour they delay, one of you will die. That should help them move.'

Diya

They bundle the other hostages back out of the room. The man's hysterical wife has to be carried by two terrorists. Salim goes with them.

He leaves and there is a silence thick with horror. I'm trying not to be sick. The sight of that man on the stairs has made my stomach churn.

Malini is holding her children and praying. I don't think I could pray. To pray, you first have to believe that God is listening. I don't think he listens at all.

Only Mr Bhonsle seems undaunted. I guess because he's drunk. 'The army is coming!' he announces loudly. 'They'll kill all you bastards. I'll kill one of you myself. With my bare hands.' Lucky man. It must be nice to have reality cushioned with alcohol and not think all of this is real. It is. It is real. And we are all going to die for real.

'It's really going to happen,' says Harish. 'We are really going to die.' It had been something we'd been worrying about. But now it is real. I look around the room, and on every face is reflected the shock of the reality of death. Coming quick, for each of us.

'I'm eighteen,' says Harish.

'Me too,' I say.

'I guess we'll never have to worry about growing old. About having backaches and things,' says Harish morosely. 'Grey hair. Having to swallow half a bottle of Digene after dinner and praying for a good crap.'

I stare at him. In the middle of all that black terror, he's worrying about a good crap. It is so unexpected, I burst out laughing. And so does Kabir.

'What?' says Harish. 'My grandmother does that.'

We just laugh harder. I think we are a little hysterical. Around the room, dazed, uncomprehending faces turn towards us.

Harish says, 'I'm only trying to look at the bright side of things. Cheer us up.'

'You have,' I say, trying to hold back the hysterical giggles that bubble out of me.

'We won't have to worry about going crazy and talking to plants,' says Kabir.

'Sprouting warts everywhere,' says Harish.

'Growing long hair out of our nostrils,' Kabir says.

'What about arthritis?' I say. 'And Alzheimer's? We won't have to worry about those things.'

'You don't have to worry about Alzheimer's,' says Harish. 'If you have it, you just forget that you're old.'

That sets us off on another round of giggles. Mr Bhonsle glares at us from his corner. He hates us. One more bonus point to dying young. We will never be bitter and angry all the time, like him.

The laughter dribbles out of us, and we go back to being silent. To waiting. 'What is the time?' asks Harish.

I look at my watch. Five minutes gone. Only fifty-five minutes left. God. How little that really is. How very small a span of time is one hour.

'If I'm going to die, I would like to die laughing,' says Kabir. 'So, did you hear about the terrorist who tried to blow up a car? He burnt his lips on the tailpipe.'

Harish and I begin to chuckle. It is crazy. It is defiant. It is our way of holding on to life even as we know death is ticking closer.

We spend the rest of the time laughing. It seems like the only thing to do. Kabir tells awful jokes. And we laugh.

Stupid. But God, how we laugh.

Kabir

There is no death. There is only me. And I am going to die.
Some great thinker said that, and I had thought it was a
really stupid thing to say, until now. I am going to die. And
that makes it real. I don't know if I care too much. It would
be a relief, I think. I only care that she will be gone.

I close my eyes and try to imagine death. Going into the
darkness. No. Death has never been darkness for me. Death
for me has been white. A white stretch of snow. Cold and
silent. A blanket for me to pull over myself and close my eyes.

The TV presenters are starting to look all tense. A babble
of worry reaches us.

'Only ten minutes remain in the deadline that the
terrorists have set . . .'

'New Delhi is yet to respond, though the prime minister
has been in a special cabinet meeting for the last forty
minutes . . .'

'All of India is now waiting as the minutes tick by . . .'

'There are only ten minutes left in the deadline that Salim Mukhtar has given for the death of another hostage . . .'

Ten minutes. And one of us in the room will be dead. I look around the room, wondering who will be chosen.

An old woman with a big heart. A security guard dying in agony. A young mother with two children. Two young and bewildered girls. An old and angry man. A young man who doesn't want to be dead. A beautiful young girl filled with sadness. And me.

Eight minutes. The screens are showing shots of people holding candles and praying. There are people in temples, in churches, in gurdwaras, and even in mosques. People on roads, linking hands and praying. They hold up placards. One of them reads, 'Killing innocent people is the problem, not the solution.' Another says, 'Spread love and peace, not guns.'

Seven minutes.

Six minutes.

Five minutes.

The damn prime minister stays silent. An election rally every day. Hours of speeches. And now, for this, he has no words.

Four minutes. 'We have a special bulletin. The prime minister has appealed to the terrorists, saying that the government is working out the details. They will respond to the demands but need one more hour.'

What is the government waiting for? Some more dead people? There are reactions to the announcement. Tears.

Two minutes. Would it be us? Or someone from one of the other groups of hostages? It seems really shitty to hope for someone else to die. Through the door, we can see Salim pacing up and down. The hostages are being held in four different rooms. Which room will he enter? Which group will win the unlucky lottery?

One minute.

Salim enters the room. It's us.

We all jerk in fright as the phones begin to ring again. Please let it be the prime minister. Let him have something to offer them.

Salim raises a hand. 'Let them ring. I think they need to know that I am very serious.'

Malini shoves her children behind her. She's praying loudly. The phones ring on and on and on.

'We need a volunteer,' Salim says. 'Anyone feel like dying?'

Nobody moves. Beside me, I can hear Harish starting to breathe so hard, he sounds like he's been running.

'Come on,' he says, smiling. 'You'll be on TV.'

He begins to walk slowly from one to the other, looking each person in the face. People cringe and look away or lower their eyes. He's enjoying this. I guess it's a kick to have people really be scared of you. Every schoolroom bully knows the feeling. I would really like to see what he's like at the other end of a gun.

'Let me see,' he says. 'Who'll play out well on TV? Tug at their heart strings? Make them cry? The young mother who leaves behind two weeping children?'

Malini scrabbles away from him, desperately holding her children to her chest.

'Or a young girl with her whole life before her?' He stops in front of the two salesgirls. They cling to each other, too afraid to even weep.

He turns to where Diya sits. 'How about a beautiful young college girl?' Diya says nothing. My heart beats faster.

He smiles at Diya. 'Has anyone told you that you really should be on TV? You have a very pretty face.'

I can't help it. I stand up. 'I'll volunteer.'

Every eye turns towards me. Salim takes his time facing me.

'Why?' he asks.

'All these people have someone waiting for them at home. I have no one to miss me.'

'Oh,' says Salim. 'Shall we take it that you're ready to die because you've been kissed?' He leans forward and whispers, 'So, who was it? I don't think it was Mother India. Or the old buddhi.'

His eyes drop to Diya and he grins. 'Congratulations. She's pretty. Worth dying for?' he asks.

I say nothing. He looks around the room, slowly and deliberately. All of us wait. Then he points. It's not to me.

His men step forward and grab one of the salesgirls: the intern. The other girl shrieks and tries to hold on to her. They have to hit her to let go. She crawls back and makes another desperate grab, and is left holding a shoe as the girl is hauled out of the door, screaming for her mother.

We turn our eyes to the screens. The entrance to the mall blinks its neon and crystal sign. The door opens, and the girl is pushed out. She runs. She runs as fast as she can across no man's land, towards the safety of the police cordon. She runs awkwardly with one high-heeled shoe off. She's halfway there when a shot rings out. Her hands jerk into the air, and she spins around and falls.

We watch it all. We can't not watch it, horrified fascination holding us wide-eyed. A group of policemen behind bulletproof shields run out and grab the body. They drag it away, and it leaves a long streak of blood in its trail.

There's a young reporter on the spot. She speaks as the body is shoved into an ambulance, the urgent wail of its siren overlapping her words. She is wearing a black armband as she says, 'Salim Mukhtar ignores the government's plea for more time. This is the second hostage who has been killed. We are told the prime minister is in an emergency meeting with the home minister and top police officials. We are expecting an announcement soon.'

Salim turns to leave the room. Then he stops and points at me. 'Majnu, you're next,' he says.

I walk back to my place and sit. Then I think I'm having a heart attack. While you're doing the stuff, you stay calm. But when it's over, your body kicks in and lets you know that it definitely doesn't appreciate a hero. It takes ten minutes for my heartbeat to get back anywhere near normal.

The last thing I expect is for Diya to be furious.

'Stop doing that!' she hisses at me. 'Stop trying to save me all the time. I don't want you dying for me. I don't want your life!'

I don't know what to say. 'I'm sorry.'

'Why do you keep doing this? You don't even know me!'

But I do.

'Let me be!' she says. 'Just leave me alone. This is a really bad time to get a crush on me, all right? I am not going to—whatever!'

I feel like I should explain. 'About the—what he was talking about—I'm sorry. It's not what you think. When he said to give him one good reason to stay alive, I told him . . . er . . . that I had never been kissed.'

That makes her fall silent. She hastily looks away. We both try our best not to look at each other. Harish is listening to us avidly.

'Me too, dude, me too!' says Harish. He looks expectantly from her to me.

'What?' asks Diya.

'You're not going to kiss him?' asks Harish. 'He just risked his life for you.'

That idiot is trying to play cupid. He couldn't have picked a worse time. I glare at him.

Diya snaps, 'No, I am not!'

'Stop it, Harish,' I say. 'Please forget it!'

'Forget it?! I'm going to die a virgin. Unkissed. Un-anythinged. This is a really good time for a girl to have pity on a guy.' He looks pleadingly at Diya. 'I mean. You would be very kind.'

Diya stares at him in a kind of angry frustration. Then, unexpectedly, she begins to laugh. 'Forget it, dude!'

I also start laughing. I know neither of us are laughing because it's funny. We're laughing because there is nothing else left to do.

Harish doesn't laugh. 'This is a bad way to die!' he says earnestly.

The TV anchor is speaking. All our heads snap towards the screen. The change in tone is so obvious. 'There has been a special communication from the Prime Minister's Office.'

She reads out a long official statement. They are going to give Salim his plane. They are going to let him get away with it.

Harish leaps up and punches the air. 'Way to go, PM!' he shouts.

The rest of us just sit there blankly. I think we're all too numb to even react.

I'm going to live. Longer than one hour. I'm going to live.

Diya

There's a chance we might get out of here alive. Salim is getting what he asked for. There will be no more killings. Malini begins thanking God loudly. I sit there, numb. I can't wrap my head around going back out of those doors. I'm not sure I want to. As long as we are here, held hostage, in this bubble, life has become simple. We are just surviving one moment at a time. There is no future worth thinking of. But now I have to think about what's next. And I can't do that. In the real world, you can't play pretend.

Strangely, the news doesn't make Mr Bhonsle happy.

'Why are they giving in? They will end up ruining this country. Terrorists will think they can get away with anything. Bah,' he mutters.

Malini turns on him. 'Don't you want to go home? What is wrong with you?'

'I care for my country, madam,' he says. 'I don't want to watch it slide into chaos.'

'They were going to kill us, and now we are going to live,' she says.

'I'm perfectly willing to die, madam,' says Mr Bhonsle. 'Better I die than the country opens the door for every man with a gun to make demands and kill innocent people.'

Who would have expected that old man to be a patriot? In that moment, he stops being a pathetic drunk and I can see the young schoolmaster filled with ideals.

'I'm going to eat my three chocolate bars in celebration,' says Harish happily.

But he hasn't made it through the second bar before everything changes again.

The TV begins airing images of a candlelight vigil outside the chief minister's bungalow. The people who have gathered are the relatives of those who had died in the train blast. They are demanding that Salim not be allowed to walk free, and are threatening to march to the mall. All kinds of organizations are announcing they will join them. Hundreds have already gathered behind the police barricades at the mall. More outraged reactions are pouring in from across the country.

Then Bhai Thakur comes on. He is spouting off at a massive rally where everyone is wearing black armbands. 'This is a government that is weak. That allows terrorists to get away. But we will teach them that there is no place for them in this country. We will send them back to where they came from. We will give them a plane, all right. One to put their dead bodies in. We will send the dead terrorists back across the border.'

The anchor comes back on the screen. 'We have a special bulletin. Some unforeseen complications seem to have arisen.'

The Directorate General of Civil Aviation has refused to give permission for the flight to take off without the filing of a proper flight plan, demanding to know who will be flying the plane. They will not let an unqualified pilot off the ground.

We sit there in shock. No. Not again. When we had finally begun to hope.

'Who is this DGCA chief?' says Harish. 'What is his problem? If the guy can't fly the plane and crashes with all the terrorists on board, it will be perfect, won't it?'

Kabir

The phones ring all together again, making us jump. Official communication. At last. Salim storms into the room and picks up one of the instruments. He never gives whoever it is at the other end a chance to speak.

'I don't want to hear anything. I don't want to hear the word complication. You now have twenty-three minutes. And then I kill someone else. After that I will kill two hostages every hour. Do you hear me?' He slams the phone down.

Twenty-three minutes.

Salim storms up and down the room, screaming. 'They think I am a fool! They think they can play me! They think they can put me back in their stinking jails. I will not go. I will kill every single hostage. And then I will take this entire place with me.'

We can see his men moving around the mall with stuff. They've pulled it out of their backpacks. Wires and some bricks of brown stuff. I know what it is. I've practised setting a bomb like that myself.

Salim turns to one of his men. 'Have you placed the explosives?'

'Yes,' says the man.

'Good. We have enough to give them a new Diwali.'

He turns to where we all sit, cringing. His voice changes and becomes the fervent tones of a priest. 'Tonight, we die. I have nothing to fear. My conscience is clear. I have done the work of God. Pray now for forgiveness all of you. Go to God clean and new.'

Everybody begins to pray. Some loudly. Some softly. The irony of it is that the terrorists pray as well. All of them praying at cross purposes. Who is God to listen to? I say no prayers. There is no God I can believe in.

Twenty minutes.

Harish's eyes keep sliding nervously to me. Even Diya constantly glances in my direction. They both know what Salim had said. I'm next.

If I believed in God, if I could have asked for something, I would have asked for forgiveness. But I know I can never be forgiven. The best I can do is atone for all that I've done.

There's one last thing I have to do. One promise I have to keep. The letter still lies against my heart. It's not sealed. I know what it says. I have read it again and again as I made my long way to her. Now it's time to hand it over.

I tap Diya on the shoulder. She turns and looks at me. I put the letter in her hand.

'What is this?' she asks.

'It's a letter. You need to have it.'

'Why?'

'Because I think this is the end. We're out of time. I know that I am next.'

She starts to shake her head and then stops. There's no point lying. She looks down at the letter. Before she can speak, Salim does. He's lost his patience.

'Come on, come on! Let's go. I want to send a message ahead of schedule. Come on, Majnu.'

Nineteen minutes.

I look away from Diya. If I see her, I won't be able to keep pretending I'm brave. I take a deep breath and get ready to stand. I hope my knees don't shake.

Jhansi ki Rani stands up. 'Shoot me,' she says.

Diya

That old lady. I don't think I'll ever meet anyone like her again. Standing there all calm, as if what she's doing is nothing special. 'My duty is done,' she says. The security guard is unmoving at her feet. He has finally slipped into death.

'It's not your turn,' says Salim. 'Sit down.'

'Oh yes, it is,' says Sharmila. 'I've been waiting to die for a while now. I think a bullet is better than a hospital bed.'

'Not you,' says Salim, turning to Kabir. 'You, boy! Get on your feet.'

Kabir stands up.

'Are you getting picky now about who you kill?' says Sharmila. 'I thought anyone would do. I'm anyone.'

'You're starting to irritate me, old woman,' says Salim.

'Good,' she says. 'Only one sure way to stop me.'

'Shut up!' shouts Salim.

'Go on, make your mother proud,' says Sharmila. 'Let her see you kill defenceless old women live on TV. Is she proud of all the widows you have made? Does she keep a count of the children?'

Salim loses it. 'Fine! Get out there, buddhi,' he says. 'I'll be glad when your mouth is shut.'

'No,' says Kabir, speaking suddenly. 'You can't do this.'

'Sit down, boy,' says Sharmila.

'No—,' says Kabir, starting forward. Two of the terrorists grab him. He tries to struggle out of their grip.

Sharmila looks at him. 'Look after my dogs,' she says. '42 Uppal Street. Matunga.'

'You can't do this! No!'

The terrorists are struggling to hold on to Kabir. One of them elbows him in the gut. He folds, but he won't stop trying to get away from them.

Sharmila walks to the door. She pauses there and smiles at us. 'Goodbye. I wish we had met under different circumstances. You seem like an interesting lot of people. I hope you survive this. If you do, live good lives.'

And with that, she walks out of the doors, her head held high.

'NO!' shouts Kabir. 'You can't do that!' He is almost weeping. A terrorist clubs him on the side of the head with his weapon. He falls into a stunned silence.

'Shut up and sit down,' says the terrorist, shoving Kabir with the butt of his gun.

Harish jumps up and grabs Kabir, forcing him to sit. Everybody turns to the bank of screens.

113

Kabir

We watch it on TV. That wonderful old woman in her kurta that is torn to strips. Stained with the blood of the dying man she had comforted. She steps out into the glare of the lights and cameras and stands there calmly. Waiting.

She falls with one bullet and does not move. She has died in my place.

How do you react to that?

I weep. I weep bitter, angry tears. Tears because I don't deserve it. Tears because someone has done something for me that I could never have imagined. Tears because I'm still alive and there's nothing for me to live for.

I don't even know when she slips her hand in mine. I look down and see I'm holding her hand. I look at our two hands intertwined. Then, gently, I put her hand away.

'I gave you a letter,' I say. 'That letter was for you.'

'A letter for me? You just met me.' She is puzzled.

'Yes. I promised I would get it to you. That is why I was following you.'

Her eyes become wary. 'From whom? What letter?'

'From Aman,' I say, watching for her reaction.

For a moment, she looks numb. Then she whispers the name. 'Aman.'

Her face lights up. 'Where is he? How is he?' She fumbles for the letter in her pocket. I lean over and hold her by the wrist before she can open it. I can feel the little vein in her wrist fluttering fast.

'I have to tell you about Aman first.'

She freezes. 'Has something happened to him?'

'Yes.'

She stares at me with frightened eyes. 'Who are you?' she whispers.

I have no choice. I tell her the truth.

'Aman is dead. And I'm the person who got him killed,' I say.

Kabir

Growing up, I didn't dream of becoming a freedom fighter. I dreamed of being the best batsman in India.

I was mad about cricket. I would be out of the house by early morning and return late in the evening, my hands sore from gripping a bat. I bunked school, broke curfews and ran away from home if I was forbidden from playing. My parents got tired of shouting at me, searching for me.

My brother always knew where to find me. He was the only one patient enough to fetch me home, make me eat and make me do my homework. He was ten years older and had a job at the local printing press. On the rare day that he had a holiday, he would join me on the cricket field. Together we would play, plan and dream. 'You have real talent,' he would tell me. 'Don't stop playing. You could play for India one day, Afzal. Imagine that!'

I dared to imagine playing for India. It was a forbidden dream, because around me the valley burnt with hatred. Young boys fought pitched battles with the police, matching bullets with stones. Everywhere there was talk of 'aazadi' for Kashmir. And I was dreaming of playing for India.

We were playing cricket one day when the world changed. My brother hadn't wanted to come along. He was tired. But I insisted. Finally, he got on his cycle, and I climbed up behind him. I had been practising, and I couldn't wait to show him my next shot.

The minute the ball touched the bat, I knew I had got it right. It was there in the crisp sound, in the way it flew off the bat. It was a six. I knew it even while the ball was in the air, and I began jumping in excitement.

At the far end of the field was a dusty path that cut across it. A jeep was driving past, and the ball headed straight for it, smashing through the windscreen. The driver lost control and the jeep swerved and rolled, spilling out the occupants. It was an army jeep. Two other jeeps behind it swerved madly to avoid a collision. Men in khaki began to emerge from those jeeps and run towards the accident.

My brother grabbed the bat from my hand. 'Run!' he said. 'RUN!'

I ran.

The army men took him away. The incident was described in the papers as terrorists attacking a military convoy. 'A young militant trained in Pakistan' had been caught.

My parents went begging from door to door. They spoke to everyone of influence they knew. My mother waited patiently outside the army camp for days, requesting anyone who came to the gates to give her news of her son. It was five days before we could even find out where he was being held.

They refused to return him to us. The charges had been made. He had simply crossed the fine line that kept ordinary Kashmiris from the chaos. He was now a 'suspected militant', and that is what he would stay for the next three years until they sent him back to us.

No one said a word to me but I knew it was my fault. I had changed everything. Most of all, my brother. When he returned, it was a stranger that the army jeep dropped off on the path in front of our house—three years after they had taken him. A stranger who stood hunched and hesitant outside the door. A stranger who cringed away from my mother's kisses, my embraces.

My mother insisted on a celebration. My father tried to stop her, but she would not listen. All the women from the neighbouring houses came to help. It was a proper Kashmiri *wazwan*, hours in the making. But when the relatives and friends began arriving, the stranger who wore my brother's face and clothes became angry. He emerged from the room he had shut himself in to stand there, stick-thin and furious. 'What are we celebrating?' he shouted. 'What is there to celebrate? That they sent me back? What about the three years they stole from me? What about what they did to me in those three years?'

My father tried to talk to him and calm him down. My brother went into his room and slammed the door.

'Let him be,' said my father. 'It will take time.'

I stood outside the door and begged. 'Bhaijaan, please open the door. Please eat something.' What I was really saying was 'please forgive me'. Forgive me for everything. Forgive me for the nights my mother wept, stifling her sobs in her *razai*. Forgive me for my father's stony silence, his blank eyes. Forgive me for the look on my mother's face as she stood day after day outside the jail walls. Forgive me for the way my father grovelled in front of people, begging, begging for his son's life. Forgive me for that moment I handed my brother the cricket bat and made him give me three years of his life in return. Forgive me. I would take it all back if I could.

Late in the night, after all the guests had left, he finally opened the door and seized both my shoulders with strong hands. 'You will never play for India,' he said. 'You will play for Kashmir one day. For aazad Kashmir.'

The seventh day after he was back, my brother took the path into the woods. It was the path taken by the angry men. The Mattoos's son had done it two years ago after a lathi charge smashed his shin and left him with a permanent limp. Two other boys from the colony had walked away one summer. My brother left on a full-moon night, the path silver in the dark.

My parents didn't say a word when they woke up to find him missing. I think they knew it was coming. They never mentioned him again. It was as if he had never existed in the story of our family. The photographs of him vanished from

119

the album. His clothes vanished from the cupboard. Only the tears remained. The secret tears my mother wept late at night. The defeated hunch of my father's shoulders.

My brother had gone, but he left me his anger. I began to look around me and see what he saw. The injustice. The callousness. The everyday humiliation. The cringing, suffocating lives we all lived. The fear that misted in every breath. My ears filled with his words. How does a man live with someone's foot on his neck? Is justice to be a fancy word written on paper, or will we make it with our own hands, our blood?

I stayed with my parents for a year. But in the end, even I took the path into the woods. My brother was waiting under the trees. He embraced me and whispered, 'We will have a new life now. We will have new dreams. You will be part of them.' I was fourteen years old. My brother was twenty-four. And we were both ready to lay down our lives for our dream.

The first time I saw Aman, he was shaking. His mouth was sealed with tape, his eyes were blindfolded, and he was shivering from the cold. His legs had been tied together so tightly with rope that it would be a couple of hours before he could even try to stand again.

'Keep him safe,' said my brother. 'If anyone finds him, we are all dead.'

'Who is he?' I asked.

'The son of a bastard,' said my brother. 'An important man.'

They left me alone with Aman in a safe house that was miles within a forest. It was the dead of winter, and we were all alone. Even I didn't dare to leave the house. A person could get lost in a matter of minutes and freeze to death in an hour.

I waited till they were long gone. I untied him and removed the blindfold. He croaked, 'Thank you.' When he tried to get to his feet, he fell over. I locked the door carefully and looked at this boy of my age, who lay there trying to smile.

Diya

The first time I ever saw Aman he was reading a book while the world around him was going crazy. The college cricket team was four runs away from beating our long-standing rivals, KC College. His friends were half laughing, half exasperated with him. With two runs to go, they took his book and flung it out into the crowd. As the winning ball touched the boundary, the crowd went mad. He had to scramble through screaming, jumping, dancing people, searching for his book.

When he went past me, I tapped him on the shoulder. 'Here,' I said, handing him the book I had rescued from between the dancing feet. He took it and said something. I couldn't hear it. The screaming of the crowd wiped away all the words between us. Shrugging, he took my hand and kissed it. Then he walked away.

I began to notice him around college. He always had a gang of friends with him. While they fooled around, passed remarks and shared jokes, he always had his head in a book. They teased him about it all the time, calling him 'Masterji', 'Kaviraj' and 'nerd'. He would just look up and smile and go back to his reading. He only ever paid attention when someone took his book away. From time to time, his friends would lose patience with him and there would be a passing match in the canteen with Aman's book.

He was surprisingly popular. Everyone seemed to know him, calling out to him as he passed by. I watched him quietly, trying to push back the memory that edged into my mind each time I saw him—a young boy casually taking my hand and kissing it in thanks.

I was alone in the canteen one day, drinking a cup of coffee, when he stopped in front of me. 'I see you're a reader as well,' he said, looking down at the book I had in front of me.

'Not like you,' I said shyly. 'That must have been a really interesting book if it kept you from watching the match.'

He looked down at me and smiled. 'Yes, it was,' he said. 'Here. Why don't you try reading it.' He dug around in his bag and handed over a battered book. It was *Palgrave's Golden Treasury of Poetry*, the second-year English text.

I laughed. 'A textbook?'

'That doesn't make the poetry any less beautiful,' he said.

He was right. His favourite poems were underlined in pencil. When I handed the book back to him, I had underlined mine.

Kabir

Iknew from the beginning that my brother was likely to kill Aman. I knew it would be stupid to like him. But try being rude to a guy who says 'thank you' for the burnt rotis and tasteless dal you shove through the door. Who wishes you good morning politely and does not seem to blame you in the least for what is happening to him. I expected him to shout and curse and abuse me and his fate. But all he did was smile and say, 'Thank you.'

The only thing that got a protest out of him was the tea. On the third morning, he put down the cup after taking one sip. 'This is really bad tea,' he said. 'Do you think I could make it?'

I hesitated.

'I'm not going to attack you or try to escape. I don't believe in violence. And there isn't anywhere to go, is there?'

I led him to the kitchen. The tea he made was strong and flavoured with ginger. Hindustani chai, not Kashmiri. We sat on the bench in the kitchen and sipped it. Ten minutes later, we were hotly arguing about Hindi film music.

'Kishore Kumar,' he said firmly. 'Mohammed Rafi. S.D. Burman.'

'They sang fifty years ago! Sonu Nigam. Arijit Singh. Atif Aslam.'

'But listen to the songs. Listen to the lyrics.' He could quote the lyrics by heart. 'When the film industry started out, they got the poets to write their lyrics. Sahir Ludhianvi, Shakeel Badayuni, Kaifi Azmi—they were real poets. And those songs are poetry set to music. That is what lyrics should be. Poetry set to music.'

He smiled shyly at me and then quoted a few lines.

What songs will you carry on your lips?
Songs of love,
Soft on the lips you kiss with.
Song of protest,
Loud on the lips you scream with.
What songs will you leave in the world,
For other lips to carry?
Everything whispers to silence.
Only the songs remain.

Aman whispered the words and I was fascinated. 'Who wrote that?' I asked.

'Me,' said Aman.

Diya

I was new in college. All of us freshers sneaked around, trying our best not to get noticed. Despite all the lectures and the rules forbidding ragging, the seniors still stopped us to make us sing and dance and do silly dares. I was petrified of being ragged, and kept my head down in the corridors.

Then my luck ran out. One day, a group of seniors surrounded me in a corridor and demanded that I sing. I stood there, gazing blankly at them, heart beating fast.

'Come on,' said a boy with wild hair standing up on end. 'Even if you can't sing, you have to. It's a fresher tax. *Lagaan*.'

I suppose they expected some Hindi film song. But I had trained as a classical singer from the time I was six years old. I put my head down, looked fixedly at my feet, and sang a thumri. When I finished, there was silence. I peeped up at them. They were all staring at me. Then the boy with wild hair jumped up. 'Come on,' he said. 'We have to take you to the auditorium.'

The others got up as well. 'Yeah. Great idea.'

They hurried me along the corridor. I went with them, not knowing what they were going to ask me to do next.

When we got to the auditorium, it was jam-packed with students. A girl was on stage, singing. She was off-key, and the audience began to howl in protest. My heart sank. I was going to be ragged in front of everyone. I spotted Aman on stage. I was going to be ragged in front of him. I wanted to turn and run, but the seniors were on either side of me.

They began to shove their way through the crowd in the aisle. They got to the front and yelled at Aman, 'Hey. We've got a good one for you.'

The boy with wild hair turned to me and said, 'Get up on stage and sing.'

I found my voice. 'I won't get on that stage,' I said. 'I'll tell the principal you're ragging me!' They looked astonished. Then they burst out laughing.

'We're not ragging you,' said one of the boys. 'We're auditioning you. These are the auditions for the college band.'

'No, no!' I said. 'I can't! I can't.' How could I explain to them that I could never sing in public? My father would never allow it.

'Can't sing?' the wild-haired boy laughed. 'We just heard you. Get up there.'

I climbed the stairs feeling like I was going to be sick. Aman looked surprised to see me. He adjusted the height of the mike.

'Go on,' he said.

The lights were blinding. The hall seemed a huge dark hole from up there. I was so scared that I closed my eyes. Then I began to sing.

There was a tremor in my voice. Somewhere along the song, a soft guitar joined me. Then another voice. A male voice. The voice steadied me. It sang with me, around me. It ran counterpoint to the harmony I was following. It lifted my voice up, and we both soared. As I felt my voice grow strong and confident, I opened my eyes. It was Aman.

Then I understood why everyone loved him. He was the lead singer with the college band. And he was really good. He always had his head stuck in a poetry book because he was trying to write his own lyrics and was fascinated with how poetry was constructed.

We sang together. Our voices joined and lifted, and the moment became magic.

How could I not fall in love?

Kabir

The second night we were out there, alone together, it began to snow. We woke up to a world that had been remade without colour. There was whiteness wherever you looked, and the sun turned everything to crystals. It was so still you could hear the trees breathing. It didn't stop for five days. There was 4 feet of snow on the ground, and we were completely cut off. No one could get through to us. It was like someone had erased the world around us.

So, we drank tea and we talked. How we talked! About love. About death. About good and evil, and why we both hated the old men who ruled our country.

I wanted to know about college. About a normal life. About how teenagers in India lived their ordinary, wonderful lives. College seemed a wonderful world of fun and hanging out. My ideas of it were drawn from Hindi films where there was never a book in sight and everyone dressed like models and did a lot of singing. He laughed when I painted this picture and said there wasn't as much singing. Even without that and with the addition of exams, it still sounded awesome to me. Mostly, I guess, because I would never make it there.

I asked a million questions. I made him describe the building, the students, the teachers. Festivals. Hanging out at the canteen. Friends. Games. The more he told me, the more I longed for his life. But I knew I could never fit in. I didn't even know what a cappuccino was. Aman saw my hunger, and he began to teach me.

There we were, in the middle of nowhere. A terrorist learning to be a gentleman from his hostage.

Aman would lay an imaginary table, and we would eat imaginary things with imaginary cutlery. He would describe the meal. 'This is an official dinner for the new superintendent of police. The menu has been printed on little cards and it's right there in front of you. We're going to begin with a prawn cocktail.'

He had already taught me what a cocktail was. But this was new. 'We're going to drink prawns?!'

'No. A prawn cocktail isn't a drink. It's a salad with prawns in it. You use the little fork to eat it.'

What sumptuous meals we had! I dined with the local MLA. With the lady Governor. I ate in five-star hotels, at fancy restaurants and at government guest houses. We even did a meal at the ambassador's residence in Moscow. Aman explained what caviar was. 'Fish eggs. The Russians love them. We got them served on boiled eggs. They were offended that I wouldn't touch mine.'

We dressed up for each dinner. With a piece of string, Aman would demonstrate how to fasten a tie. My shawl would become a coat. An achkan. An overcoat with a fur collar that he'd once worn on a short trip to Moscow in the winter.

We hung out at his college. He described all his friends as they joined us. We sat in his class and listened to his professors. He taught me fads, slang, what was in and what was old and dead.

I borrowed his life, and he let me. He made me a gift of it and just watched me with those sad eyes of his as I tried it on for size.

Amanbhai. I don't know when it slipped out of my mouth. But it seemed so correct, it was what I called him after that. We were unlikely brothers.

Then one day, he told me about her.

'So, do you have a girlfriend?' I couldn't resist asking. Aman was silent for a long time. Then his eyes lit up in a slow smile.

'Yes,' he said. 'And she has me.'

'What is she like?'

He took some time to reply. 'The first time I saw her, people were going crazy around her—shouting, jumping, dancing. And she was standing still, a smile on her face. That's what she is, really. Still. Calm. A small, peaceful space where the world vanishes and I can just stop and rest.' His love for her was dancing in his voice. 'She doesn't talk much. But when she sings. Ah. It's like she's breathing in air and breathing out light. It is so beautiful.'

I was listening, entranced. 'Is she beautiful?'

'Yes. Very beautiful. But when you really love someone, it doesn't matter what they look like. It's them that you love. She's beautiful inside and outside.' He smiled and softly said the words of one of his poems.

What is God?
A paltry thing.
When she laughs
He slips from my mind
And is gone.

I was jealous. I too wanted a love like that. A girl whose laughter shook everything, even God, from my mind.

Diya

I wanted to sing with Aman again. I wanted so much to share the flow that we had found together. But first, I had to ask my father for permission to sing. For three long days, I just couldn't work up the courage. Then, I told myself, what was the use of asking a question to which I already knew the answer?

It was difficult getting Aman on his own. He was always surrounded by friends, but I knew I had to speak to him before rehearsal began. I finally walked up to him as he sat reading under a tree. He looked up at me and smiled. 'It's the girl with the voice like sunshine.'

'I can't sing,' I said, blurting out everything I wanted to say in one nervous rush. 'I mean, I won't be allowed to. I can't be part of the band. I can't come for rehearsals. My father won't allow me. I'm sorry.'

Aman kept looking up at me. 'Do you like singing?'

'Of course,' I said.

'Do you sing for your father or yourself?'

'For myself. I love it. It makes me happy.'

'Don't give up on something you love so easily.' He was looking at me as he said it. 'Happiness is not so easy to find.'

I thought about that for a long time. With his words, it came home to me that my life was small and poor. There had been so little happiness in it. There had been plenty of duty. My mother had taught me that, because that was all that she had. No love. No happiness. Do your duty and watch life pass by.

Even the music I loved was given to me because my father thought classical music lessons would make me better marriage material. Instead, they became the one thing that held my hand and led me through my days. I couldn't let go.

Eventually, after thinking and worrying about it for hours, I invented an extra class that took place after college. When I walked through the door for the first rehearsal, Aman smiled at me. Looked up and smiled. Then it hit me—there was one more thing that gave me happiness. Him.

Kabir

Just before my brother was taken away, I had started to discover girls. Well, this one girl. She was a neighbour, and two years older than me. But she had this way of giggling that sounded so friendly and so happy. I would watch her going off to school with her sister. I would make sure to be busy outside when she came back. I just watched, and when she looked at me, I would look the other way. It made her giggle. And listening to her laughter made me happy.

Then, our world changed. She stopped me once, after my brother had been taken by the army. She started to say how sorry she was, but I just walked away and left her standing there.

After I joined my brother, I had barely seen a girl. I mean, I had passed them on streets when we were in the city. But we were mostly hiding in one place or the other. And even those who hid us and sympathized with us hid their daughters before they let us into their homes.

I hadn't spoken to a girl in years. I'd learnt many things. Firing a gun. Putting together crude petrol bombs. Strategies for killing. Strategies for staying alive. But girls? I'd learnt absolutely nothing about them. I didn't even know what I'd say if I got a chance to talk to one. The only thing I could talk about was aazadi.

Aman didn't find it funny when I said that. He looked sad. 'You're eighteen. This is not the life you should be living. At this age you shouldn't be knowing how to patch an exit wound. Or how to kill a man. You should be worrying about girls. And pimples. Crap like that.'

'I do worry about girls,' I said. 'I worry that I know nothing about them. And that I'm never going to.'

'A relationship between a girl and a boy is the most beautiful thing. You have a right to discover it. With this life you never will, Afzal.'

'I will find myself a girlfriend!'

'Where? Running from safe house to safe house? When you go to town to throw bombs? This is not the life you should be living.'

'I have chosen it,' I said. 'I'm a patriot. A freedom fighter.'

'Whose freedom are you fighting for by giving away your own?'

'This is my choice!' I said.

'Is it really?' he asked softly.

'Yes. I choose to fight for aazadi. With aazadi, a new life will begin for my people. We will no longer be under the tyranny of those who despise us. Who kill us!'

'Are these your words? Are these truly your words?'

'Yes. I have seen the injustice myself. I have seen my brother suffer. All Kashmiris are my brothers. I want justice. I want freedom. I will die for it!' My voice faltered and stopped. I realized these were my brother's words. His beliefs, not mine. What did I really want?

And the answer slid into my mind. A cup of coffee. Just a simple cup of coffee. Because to be sitting in a cafe drinking a cup of coffee was a freedom that I had never known. A personal freedom. And it beckoned me more strongly than the freedom my brother talked of. One simple cup of coffee. And maybe someone across the table smiling at me as I sipped it.

Even as I thought it, I knew it could never be. I was paying a debt to my brother by handing my life to him. But it would never balance things out. The debt was too big and made up of too much pain. I could never leave.

Diya

Music. And Aman's smile. Two little pieces of stolen happiness that lit up my days. I loved the rehearsals. They were a light in my life. But Aman insisted I was the light. I was the sunshine. That's what he used to call me: 'sunshine'. He said that when I stopped singing, the sun went behind clouds and the day became dark.

I loved it the most when the two of us sang together. Aman loved experimenting with fusion, mixing western jazz and Indian classical. He sang in English and I sang in Hindi. Yet, when our two voices came together, it always sounded amazing. The rest of the band began to get excited about it as well. We had to start locking the doors of the auditorium because so many people wanted to hear what we were doing.

One day, we were rehearsing when someone began hammering on the door. Aman hated the rehearsals being disturbed, but the knocking wouldn't stop. An extremely angry Aman finally flung open the door. His friends swarmed in and began singing 'Happy Birthday', laughing when he tried to throw them out. They wanted to carry Aman off with them, but he refused to go. 'Rehearsals first,' he said. 'We're working hard here.' They left reluctantly, demanding a treat. We went back to practising. But when we were packing up, Aman held back.

'What's the matter?' I asked him.

'I really don't want to celebrate,' he said. 'I don't like the fuss that's made over a birthday.'

'Why not? It's nice to have a birthday celebration.'

He looked at me with sadness in his eyes. 'It's not just my birthday. It's also the day my mother died.'

I was stunned into silence. 'What would you like to do?' I asked.

'Run away,' he said.

'Come on,' I said on an impulse. 'Let's do that. Let's run away.'

We ducked out of the hall from the backstage entrance. 'Come, I'll show you my secret place,' said Aman.

I was surprised when he led me to the little chapel that stood in one corner of the campus. There were wooden steps that led up into a belfry. Below the dusty bells, there was a wooden platform and a small window with a view of the campus.

We weren't the first to discover the place. The platform was covered with names of couples carved deep into the wood. Some of them had carved dates. Lovers had been coming here for eighty years.

The space was tiny, and our knees touched as we settled down.

'Now what do we do?' I asked.

He laughed, 'Did you really have to ask? You know me.' He pulled a book out of his backpack. 'I've got a new book of love poems.'

He read to me, and lovers down the ages spoke to us of their joy and their pain. Then we just sat there in silence, content to be with each other, reading the names on the floor.

'I didn't know it was your birthday. I don't have a present to give you,' I said.

He smiled at me. 'You could give me your hand.'

I didn't know how to react. In a moment of blind panic, I decided to pretend I hadn't heard him. He waited for a moment. Then he found a new page and continued reading. I looked at his hand, lying there casually, within reach.

I pretended to move and brushed against it. Then, trying my hardest to make it look casual, I sort of slipped my hand into his very warm one. For a second or two, he didn't respond, and I really thought he was too busy reading to notice. Then his hand tightened on mine, and he looked into my eyes.

'Best present ever,' he said softly.

Kabir

'Have you even held a girl's hand?'

I refused to admit I hadn't, but it was written all over my face. Aman didn't laugh. 'It's beautiful. You reach out. You don't know if she is going to give you her hand. You wait, heart beating. Then her hand nudges yours. Her fingers brush lightly, so lightly, against yours. And suddenly your hand is filled with warmth. You are holding her hand. Girls have hands that are so soft.'

He smiled at my rapt expression. 'It's beautiful, because it's not her hand she's giving you. It is her trust.'

I had never let myself think too far ahead. I never let myself actually think of a future. But now I began to wistfully wish that one day I could hold somebody's hand.

'Have you ever kissed a girl? I mean . . . did you . . . with her?'

Aman grinned at me. 'If I refuse to tell you, it's going to drive you crazy, isn't it?'

'No, I'm cool.' I said, practising how to talk like a college kid.

Aman gave a chuckle. 'Sure.'

'Oh, come on!' I said. 'Just tell me.'

But he wouldn't. He really made me sweat for the story. He only told it to me late at night when sadness came upon him.

Diya

We would sit in the bell tower almost every day. It had become our own special space. Hidden away from the world, we sat and talked. Sometimes we sang. One day, we were holding hands and I was humming to him. When I stopped, he protested.

'Don't stop singing. I love to hear you.'

'Sing along,' I said. 'I like it best when we both sing.'

'But I am,' he said. 'My heart sings every time it sees you. It's singing right this moment. Can't you hear it?'

'No,' I said, laughing.

'I bet I can make you hear it,' he said with a wicked twinkle in his eye.

'I'm not coming any closer.'

'No, no. Stay where you are. But close your eyes. And listen.'

I closed my eyes, laughing, and waited. Then the most extraordinary sound filled the tiny space. It was a hum that grew and grew and vibrated through the air. I opened my eyes in surprise. Aman had knocked on the bell and was running a pencil around the rim. It made the bell hum. He began to hum along with it. Just a simple hum, but it was magical.

'Do that again,' I said, entranced. And he did. As the hum wove around us, he smiled at me and whispered a poem.

> Who knows what the sound
> of a heart song is?
> Only your God
> And your beloved.

He slid closer to me. And closer. The hum died away, and there was silence. We were less than an inch apart. We stayed that way, suspended in silence. Then I leaned forward and put my lips on his.

His lips were soft and warm and stroked gently along mine. Slowly, so slowly, he taught me to kiss, one gentle nuzzle at a time. Then we were really kissing. Deep and slow and long.

Kabir

I woke up to the sound of something clattering in the kitchen. Aman was making us breakfast. There weren't any vegetables left. We were living on dal and chapattis. He fried the chapattis and sprinkled them with salt. We ate them with pickle, and they were delicious.

We were entirely cut off from the world. I would later learn that across those six days Kashmir got the heaviest snowfall it had seen in sixty years. Even the little radio I had was dead. The batteries were gone, and I didn't have any extra ones. The electricity had gone on the first day, when wires snapped under the weight of snow. I had been unable to charge my mobile. A curtain of snow had descended between us and the rest of the world. There was just Aman and me. It was actually the happiest time I had spent in the last five years.

We spent the morning playing *antakshari*. He beat me completely. He knew about a million songs more than me. Then I tried to get the topic back to him and her. I needed to know. I really needed to know.

'So, what happened, Amanbhai? Why is she in Mumbai and you in Kashmir? What happened? Why aren't you together?'

'Real life isn't a film. Girl meets boy. Comedy. Tragedy. Remedy. Happy ending.' He shook his head.

'You didn't have a happy ending?'

He grinned, 'Picture abhi baaki hai, yaar. We got to the bit where the families object.'

Diya

We wrote each other letters. While everyone else sent emails and text messages, Aman wrote beautifully on thick paper. He wanted us to have something that we could hold on to for all our lives. 'I want this to be forever. I want us to have every minute, always,' he said.

Passing the letters to each other was a game. Sometimes they reached me under a bench. Sometimes he passed them as he brushed past me in the corridor. Sometimes I followed the direction of his eyes and saw a letter tucked in an unexpected place.

I would fold a letter up tight and tuck it into my hairband. I would casually drop it on his table as I walked past him in the canteen. I would fan myself with it elaborately and then leave it lying around for him to claim.

I would carry his letters all day long, not opening them. Savouring them, waiting till I was alone in bed at night.

Then, after reading them, I would breathe the words to myself, repeating them in the darkness. He wrote me poetry. He took all that he felt and put it into words on the page. And I took them and sang them back to him. At the rehearsals, they marvelled at the stuff he was coming up with. And he and I looked at each other and smiled.

Until my father took all the letters. I never saw them again. I think he must have burnt them. Happiness makes us careless. I forgot that my father watched me carefully. Forgot that he notices things.

The last night of the college festival, I asked him for permission to stay over at a girlfriend's house. It was likely to be late. All the girls had planned this. There would be many of us, and no boys. He agreed. I should have known it was too easy. I was just too happy to realize it.

Kabir

I made a really large fire. I didn't want to have to get up for wood before the story was over. We sat in front of it, draped in blankets. Aman told me of the night it all changed for them.

'Our college festival is famous. It's really big. Three days of events across fifteen different areas. Everything, from debates to art to fashion shows. But the biggest day is the last day, when all the bands take to the stage. The concert lasts the whole night. Last year it went on till 4 a.m. and the cops had to come and shut it down.

'We'd been rehearsing a long time. And we were good. We were going to do a song that I had written, and it made me really nervous. I had written the song for her, and I would be telling a crowd of thousands about my love.

'Before we went on stage, I was ambushed. My friends got together and grabbed me. Then they threw me into the air three times. They said it was for luck. I was breathless and laughing as I flew into the air and landed in their arms again and again. As I was flung above their heads, I could see the crowd. There were four thousand teenagers packed into the auditorium. I could hear them roaring. This was going to be incredible.'

Diya

I was almost light-headed with tension. My hands were cold. Putting on my make-up, I looked in the mirror and wondered who this girl was who was suddenly ready to rebel. I was defying my father. Singing in public. Lying about where I was. And I was going to spend the night with my boyfriend.

I can't tell you how terrifying it was to think that after this night, I would have crossed a line my father would never ever forgive me going past. But I was ready. Happiness had come to me, and it had made me think of freedom. I would not be my father's pawn, married to whomever he chose. I would not do my duty. I was in love, and I would do what my heart wanted.

'Happiness is hard to come by. Don't give up on it so easily,' Aman had said. And I had learnt that you could make your own happiness, hold on to it. You just had to be ready to pay the price. I was. On that night, I was.

My girlfriends surrounded me. I had made so many friends since I started rehearsals. They helped me do my hair. Fixed my lipstick. We were all laughing and chattering.

Moniya squeezed my hand tight. 'I won't tell a soul,' she said. She was the girl who had volunteered to pretend that I was at her house that night. 'Where are you going?' she asked.

I had no idea. I had left it all to Aman. There was a knock on the dressing room door. Aman was standing there. 'Come on, sunshine,' he said. 'It's time to light up the night.'

He held out his hand. Mine was cold. His was warm. He was holding my hand as we walked on to the stage.

So many people. I was suddenly hit by the reality of it. So many people. And me in front of them. I felt my throat close up.

Kabir

The fire crackled and sputtered. But I wasn't in a small wooden house in the middle of nowhere. I was far away in a crowd, watching a stage bathed in bright lights. Watching as a boy and girl walked on to it.

'And then?' I said to Aman.

His eyes were shining. He shook his head. 'It was almost a disaster. I saw her freeze. Saw her hear the opening music, look at the crowd and just freeze. I stepped forward and gently touched her shoulder. She began to breathe again. Then she started singing.

'You should have seen that crowd. Huge. Noisy. Uncontrollable. And then she began to sing, and all the noise slowly began to die down. Her voice did that. I think the whole hall was holding its breath. By the time I joined her in singing, they were listening to us. Really listening. We had them.

'We sang a song that I had written. I wrote it for her.'

The stars you named,
Became ours forever,
They watch in a still dark sky.
The love you named,
Can leave me never,
It can never die.

I will count the stars as I wait for you,
And make the whole sky ours.
This world is not enough to hold
Our love, so we reach for stars.

Diya

The hall erupted. They yelled and screamed and clapped. They wouldn't let us get off the stage. We had to sing three more songs before they would let us go.

We didn't even wait for the results. Aman said, 'We've won. Let the others collect the trophy. We have something more important to do.' He grabbed my hand, and we dodged all our friends who were screaming in excitement, and ran for the exit. We had to fight our way out of there.

Aman had borrowed a motorcycle from a friend. I began to tie up my hair, but he pulled the rubber band from me. 'Never tie your hair up,' he said. My hair blew behind us as we rode that bike. I put my arms around his waist and leaned into him. He smelt so good. Only the two of us, warm against each other, and the speeding bike.

They caught us just off Peddar Road. A car full of men. They forced us to the side of the road and then jumped out, sticks in hand. Two of them grabbed me. The others grabbed Aman. He tried to fight free, but they held him easily. He yelled to me, 'Run away! Run away, Diya!'

I didn't move. I had recognized them, and there was no place to run. My father's secretary was with them. He smiled at me as the goons held Aman and me.

'I know them,' I said to Aman.

'You know them?!'

'Yes. They're my father's men.'

'Don't touch her!' shouted Aman. 'Don't you dare hurt her!' His only concern was for me. But I was terrified for him. I knew my father.

The secretary said politely, 'Don't worry about her. We aren't going to touch her. We're here to beat a lesson into you.'

'You want to beat me up?' said Aman. 'You're not going to harm her?'

'No. Our orders are that we don't touch her. She is like a daughter to us. You, however . . .' The secretary smiled. His politeness was chilling.

'All right,' said Aman. And then he just stood there. The lead thug smashed his fist into Aman's face. Aman just took the blow and stood there waiting. He didn't do a thing.

Kabir

There was only one thing wrong with Aman. Gandhi.

I never knew anyone who had a worse case of Gandhi than Aman. He had read every single book the man had written. He could quote him, analyse him, memorize him. I put it down to his father being in the business of violence. He told me the story.

Aman's earliest memory was of his father returning from a lathi charge. The front of his uniform was splattered with blood. Aman began crying, thinking that his father was hurt. But it was the blood of other people.

Aman stumbled upon Gandhi accidentally when his father was transferred to Moradabad. His mother was dead by then. The city was in the middle of riots, so his father kept him at the police station during the day to keep him safe.

Tired of waiting through the day for his father to return from riot duty, he began reading the books in the police

157

outpost. There were twelve volumes of Gandhi's writings on one small shelf. They were covered with dust and a couple had been eaten by termites. No one had ever read them. But Aman read them with fascination, asking the policemen for help with the big words.

His father would come back late at night after dealing with the riots all day. He never talked about what he did. The next morning, Aman would read about it in the papers. The fatalities. The blood that flowed in the gutters. How many bullets the police had fired. Sometimes there were pictures of those who had been gunned down.

He began to dread sitting down with his father. He watched him wash his hands before dinner and wondered whose blood was on those hands. He tried to talk about Gandhi to his father, tried to tell him about the strange, exciting ideas that were flooding his head.

His father laughed. 'Gandhi. We salute him twice a year. And every day we do everything he told us not to, just to keep this country going.'

His father had become a man whose only answer was violence. That was all his life had come down to. He was paid to be a last stand. A butt against the head. A bullet through the brain.

It was not his father's choices, but Gandhi's principles which began to make sense to Aman. By the time the riots ended, Aman had that man inside his head for good.

How we argued, Aman and I.

I could understand hating violence. But worshipping Gandhi? Well, okay, he got us freedom and all that. But what did his non-violence get him? Three bullets in the chest from someone who disagreed with him. Bullets beat bhajans every time.

But try telling that to Aman. Gandhi was his God. How we fought.

'You must become the change you want to see in the world,' said Aman. 'You want a more peaceful world? Then you stop being a terrorist.'

'If I stop, will everyone else stop? Will the army no longer beat up people in the street? Will riots stop? How can one person change anything?'

'All the change you can ever make is in one person. Yourself. You want change? Start with yourself. Put the gun down.'

In that instance, he meant it literally. We were outside in the cold. I had set up a tin can as a target and was practising my aim. With every shot, the birds rose into the sky, chirping away frantically.

'And that will solve everything?'

'As long as you have a gun in your hand, you are part of the problem.'

'It's not me!' I said, hitting the can and making it skip through the snow. 'I never started this. They forced me to take this path.'

'No,' said Aman. 'It was your choice. You didn't have to reply to hatred with hatred. If even one person chooses not to reply with violence, things will change.'

I laughed at him as I set up the target again. 'Gandhi is dead,' I said. 'If he had lived, there would have been no place for him in this world.'

'He is alive. They killed the man, not what he stood for. Otherwise why are we arguing about him? There is a place for him. The day there is no place for love and compassion in this world, the world will die.'

I kicked the can and looked around. The world looked pristinely white, as if it had been made anew. As if there were no darkness, no rottenness anywhere at all.

'They held my brother. They tortured him. And he had done nothing. Someone has to pay!' I said.

'An eye for an eye can only make the whole world blind, Afzal,' said Aman softly.

I couldn't think of an answer to that one.

'Look at you,' he said, 'stuck in the middle of nowhere. With a gun for company. Practising to kill. Can you really aim it at someone and kill them?'

'If I have to. Yes.' I aimed and shot. He had made me so mad, I missed.

Aman waited till the flat echoes of the shot had died. 'No, you can't,' he said. 'You are not a violent person. You cannot kill.'

'I can!' I said.

He smiled and shook his head. 'One day, a moment will come when you will be asked to kill—and you won't be able to. Then you will realize the truth about yourself.'

'I know the truth about myself,' I said. I held up the gun. 'This is my truth. I will use it when I have to.'

'On me?' said Aman. 'What if you had to use it on me?' He walked up to me, grabbed the barrel and placed it on his chest.

I pushed him away.

'You can't shoot me because we've become friends. But think how every stranger is someone's friend. Every stranger is a person like you. Who hopes. Who loves. Who is afraid. Who wishes he could hold a girl's hand. Who all will you kill?'

I wrenched the gun away and walked back to the house. Aman followed me, still talking. 'You have borrowed your brother's truths. One day, you will understand that violence is not the answer and can never be.'

'It is the answer,' I said. 'I will kill if I have to. The day I let down my brother will never come.'

'Oh yes, it will,' he said, smiling. 'One day, you will know you cannot kill. Then you can start your life again.'

It was an argument that went on for several days. Aman could be incredibly stubborn when he chose to be. In his own quiet way, he was very persistent. We returned to it again and again.

His insistence made me angry. It made me furious that he thought I wasn't man enough to pull that trigger.

'Gandhi,' I said bitterly. 'His ideas have turned your head.' We were on the roof, shovelling the snow off it. It had started to creak and groan under the weight of the snow, and I was afraid it would collapse.

'That man helped me make sense of the world,' said Aman. He shook his head. 'God, it made my father crazy.'

Aman finished reading the Gandhi books and started a non-cooperation movement of his own at home. He was twelve. His father was part of an elite hit squad that was sent in to handle difficult situations. He wanted his father to get out of the business of being an official killer. So, he went on a hunger strike. His father raged, shouted, argued. Then he decided to ignore Aman, figuring that his son wouldn't be able to keep it up.

Aman lasted seven days. On the seventh day, his father came home to find him passed out near the door. He took Aman to hospital, where Aman refused to let the doctors touch him. When they put him on a drip, he pulled it out. Finally, they had to tie him to the bed.

His father walked into the room and saw his son tied to the bed. He just turned around and walked out again, returning with a cup of ice cream. Aman refused to eat it.

'Why?' asked his father for the umpteenth time.

'You're all I have left. I don't want you to be a killer.' Aman hesitated before he said the next words. 'And I don't want you to die.'

His father sighed and began undoing the knots holding him in place. 'Come on,' he said. 'Eat the ice cream. I'll apply for a transfer tomorrow. But I will not leave the police.' It was a bittersweet victory for Aman. But he never gave up the fight. He had spent years locked in a struggle with his father, both of them too stubborn to give up.

I never believed in Gandhi. I never thought his words worked in the real world. 'All you know is theory. Theory and high ideals you read in a book. What do you know about violence? About being beaten up?'

'I've stood there and let someone beat me up,' said Aman. 'I had to have six stitches.'

'You?' I said disbelievingly.

'It's not easy to stand there and let someone hit you,' said Aman. 'But I had a choice between reacting like everyone else. Or living by my real beliefs.'

That was when he told me about the bike ride.

'I like bikes,' said Aman. 'I hadn't really thought of where I was going to take her. We just rode. She put her arms around my waist, and her hair kept blowing into my face. It smelt of lemons. God, both of us were so happy and so free.'

He shrugged. 'I will always remember that bike ride. It was the last time the two of us were simply and happily together.'

A car had come up behind them and forced them to the side of the road. It drove so recklessly that Aman had to stop his bike. The doors opened and the goons poured out. They went to grab Diya. Aman fought to get them off her.

Diya

Gandhi. All his friends teased Aman saying that he was the last Gandhian. I knew how much he admired the old man, but I didn't realize how serious he was about nonviolence until I watched him stand there and take a fist in the face.

The leader of the gang of thugs punched him. Aman took the blow without flinching. I tried to get to him but they held me back. I screamed and fought. And Aman just stood there while he was hit again and again.

'This one is a smart-ass,' said the leader. 'He's going to need some more teaching.'

He nodded at the other men. One of them stepped forward and jammed a stick into Aman's stomach.

I screamed. I kicked. I was so petrified. Aman fell to the ground.

The secretary asked politely, 'Her father doesn't want you near her. You going to stay away from her now?'

'Will you beat me if I don't?' asked Aman, struggling to get his breath back.

'I'm afraid so. You see, you have to learn your lesson and learn it well.'

'I'm not going to stay away from her.'

'Go!' I begged Aman. 'Leave me and go!' He just looked at me and got back on his feet.

'This guy is a slow learner. Let's teach him a good lesson.' The secretary nodded to the men with him. They began beating up Aman with sticks. He made no attempt to defend himself or to fight back; he just fell to the ground, curled up and tried to save his head. He began to bleed.

'NO!' I screamed. 'If you hurt him any more, I will hurt myself. I will take a knife and cut my wrists. You tell my father that.' It was the only thing I could think of. And I meant it.

The secretary turned to look at me. Then he pulled out his phone and dialled a number. He held the phone to my ear.

'Papa, listen to me,' I said. 'You can't watch me every second of every day. I will find a time and I will hurt myself. The more you hurt him, the more I will hurt myself. You want me to get married? I'll burn my face. You'll never find anyone to get me married to. Listen to me, Papa!'

There was a long silence. No one threatens my father. In my desperation, I tried.

Then my father said, 'Hand the phone over.' He gave instructions. One of the men shoved me into their car. I tried to fight my way back to Aman but they wouldn't let me. The last sight I had of him was him lying on the ground as they beat him. I had no idea if they were going to let him live.

I screamed as loudly as I could, 'I love you! Aman, I love you!' Then the car started, and I was driven away.

Kabir

They didn't kill Aman. But they beat him mercilessly. Then they took him to a police station. They told the officer on duty that he had been caught teasing a girl. 'Must be the spoilt son of some rich father,' said the officer. 'What is your father's name?'

Aman was grinning as he told the story. 'It was really hard to smile because they had bust my lip and my jaw was swollen. But I couldn't help laughing. I said, "My father's name is Prem Shourie, DGP North Mumbai."'

I gave a shout of laughter. 'Shabash! Your father was the DGP?! Fuck! What happened then?'

'The officer in charge almost had a heart attack. He sent a constable running off for the first-aid kit. But it only had some cotton and a bottle of mercurochrome. He yelled at the men who had brought me in, *"Marwayega kya?"* They vanished very quickly. Then my father arrived.

'He didn't say anything. We got in the car and drove away. He took me straight to a doctor who patched me up. I had to get six stitches in my eyebrow. I lost a couple of teeth and had three broken ribs.

'Then my father asked if I would like to have an ice cream. There was no way I could have had an ice cream with the state of my mouth, but it was our childhood code. Whenever I needed comfort, my father had bought me an ice cream.

'We took the car to Marine Drive and found a spot on the rocks. Then I sat there, watching my ice cream melt as my father tried to talk to me. We were talking after years. It wasn't easy for either of us.

"So, the girl is in your college?" he asked.

"Yes," I said, through swollen lips and broken teeth.

"Did you know who her father is?"

"Yes. You could say I was reminded the hard way today," I said. I waited for the lecture but it never came.

"Is it any use to tell you to stay away from the girl?" he asked.

"No," I said.

'To my surprise, my father began to laugh. "This is me and your mother all over again." He told me their story. He never talked about my mother. He had never told me a thing about how they met and got married. I always thought they had a boring arranged marriage. Turns out it was way more interesting than that.

'My father was the local goonda. He and his friends used to hang around the locality, organizing all the festivals and the football tournaments. Once, my mother's cycle got a puncture right at the edge of the football field. His father ran the local repair shop. When she went to the shop, my father fixed the puncture for her and promptly fell in love.

'My grandfather refused to let his daughter have anything to do with the useless local boy. He tried to get her married to someone else.

'But my father then turned up at that boy's house and told him if he dared to marry her, he would break his legs. After that, my grandfather found that no one was willing to marry his daughter.

'So, my father went over and suggested he let them marry. The old man said he would only give her to someone respectable. Then my father asked, "What is respectable enough for you?"

"Someone who puts people like you behind bars," my grandfather replied. So my father went to my mother and asked her if she would wait five years. She said yes.

'He sat for the civil services exam. Went off for IPS training. The day he got his uniform, he went to the old man and saluted him. "Now am I acceptable?" he asked. To his credit, my grandfather kept his word and let them marry.

'All these years and my father had never told me the story. I had a sudden vision of him, young and reckless and in love. I liked it.

'My sober, stable, respectable father looked at me and sighed. "You're too young," he said.

"How old were you when you met Mum?" He was silent. "You've forgotten, Dad. Try to remember what it was like."

'He sighed. His voice was very sad. "I made myself forget. I loved your mother very much. I couldn't bear it when I lost her."

"Me too," I said. We were both silent for a while. I mushed the ice cream in the bottom of the cup. He finished his.

"So, what are we going to do now?" I asked.

"Go and ask her if she will wait five years," he told me.

"She will," I said. "I don't have to ask to know."

"Then let us see what happens next," he said.

'A great happiness filled my heart. I had my father's support. It was worth getting beaten up to have got that.'

I looked at Aman and didn't say what was in my own heart. I would have taken a hundred beatings to have my father's support. I would have taken more to see my mother one more time.

Diya

My father faced me the morning after the festival. He looked at me with contempt, then turned to my mother. 'See your daughter. This is what you taught her? To lie to her parents. To run around with boys.'

My mother said nothing. But I did. 'Don't blame her,' I said. 'Whatever I did, I did myself.'

My mother's eyes widened. I had never talked back to him. She looked at me in fear.

He slapped me hard. 'You children of today,' said my father. 'You sing one song with a boy, and you imagine that you are in love with him.'

'I do love him,' I said. He slapped me again, so hard that my lip split and blood began to fill my mouth.

'Enough!' said my father. 'I don't want to hear that word from your mouth. You go near him again in college, and

I will make sure you leave your studies and get married within a month.'

I said nothing. There was no point. I didn't want Aman to get hurt again. My mother pleaded with me with her eyes to be quiet. Afterwards, she washed my cut lip and told me to forget Aman.

'Please,' she begged. 'You know what he's like. You can't go against him. He would never allow it.'

'Maybe *you* can live your whole life without love,' I said. 'I can't.'

When Aman came back to college, he had a limp. His right eye was swollen shut. All his friends looked at me strangely. I could see they blamed me. But he didn't.

We first saw each other in the canteen. Aman smiled through swollen lips and began to limp towards me. I shook my head. On either side of me sat two men. My father had sent them to guard me. The principal had thrown a fit, but my father was not a man to be denied.

I shook my head. I pleaded with my eyes. I could not have borne to see him beaten up again. Aman understood. He stood in front of me for a long, long moment. On either side of me, the men tensed. Then he turned and limped back to a bench on the other side of the room.

He got a cup of coffee. I did the same. Then he sat across the room and drank it. He locked eyes with me and never broke the gaze. For every sip he took, I took a sip too. We were in a crowded canteen. But we could have been entirely alone, sharing every breath. There was pin-drop silence. Everyone was watching us.

Then the smiles began. Right across that canteen there were smiles as we drank our coffee together, as close as it is possible for two people to be. People smiled and we drank our coffee, matching each other sip for sip. Each sip a declaration of love.

I understood that Aman was right. Victory doesn't come from violence or strength. Victory can be as simple as a cup of coffee. A smile across a room. Freedom is in the small things. And no one can take those from you.

Kabir

'So, you drank coffee and smiled at her across a room. That didn't make her yours. It didn't change anything.'

Aman smiled. 'She was already mine. And nothing they did could change that. They can beat you. They can separate you. But who can stop you from loving?'

He made me really mad. 'I would have run away with her. I would not have let those men beat me. I would have picked up my gun.'

Aman shook his head. 'There is only one freedom. The freedom of choice. You can choose your response to anything. You can respond with anger, revenge and violence. Or you can respond with understanding and compassion. That is the only choice there is.'

'But you couldn't be together.'

'My love is not so shallow that it cannot wait. I'm willing to wait for her. She is waiting for me. We will be together one day.'

'Then why are you here in Kashmir? Where is she?' I asked. I had to know.

Aman turned away from me. The shadows came back into his eyes.

'A week after the night of the bike ride, she vanished.'

Diya

He vanished.

I went away, and when I came back, he was gone.

A week after Aman was beaten up, I got into the car waiting for me outside the college and found my mother sitting there, waiting for me. 'What are you doing here?' I asked.

She tried to smile. 'We are going to see your grandmother. She is not well.'

Lies. I knew what was happening. I was being taken away from him. They didn't know how to stop us loving each other. My minders must have reported to my father. And this was his solution: send her to jail.

The village my father came from was a remote one in the middle of Maharashtra. It made for a perfect jail without bars. My phone was taken away. There was no question of an Internet connection. I was watched day and night. In

176

the other room, my grandmother muttered endlessly in her dementia that got worse every day. My mother talked to me, trying to convince me that I was wrong to go against my father. I told her to be quiet. It was my life to waste. I would not do what she had done and give my life to a man to whom it meant nothing.

Every day I wept, I argued, I fought. A month later, when I was allowed to come back, Aman was gone. His father had been transferred to Kashmir. He had gone with him.

When I logged in to my email account, there was a mail from him for every day we had been apart. He had sent me a poem every single day. The last mail was sent three days before I returned. His phone was now switched off. There was no reply to the endless mails I sent him. None of his friends knew where he had gone. None of them could help me contact him. He was gone from my life. I only had his words.

> We can never be apart
> No matter the distance
> I go away closer
> My breath goes into the world
> And calls your name
> When I count the stars
> Each one
> Is you and you and
> You
> Are always there.

Kabir

I stared at Aman in surprise. 'Vanished? Where did she go?'
Aman shrugged. 'No one knew. None of her friends.
I tried calling her house. I even got her father's number. No
one ever took my calls. I tried waiting outside her house.
Nothing. Her phone was switched off. She didn't reply to
any mails. After two days, I went to my father.

'I just walked in on him having a meeting with a whole
lot of top brass. I stood there while he told them to go away.

"What is it, beta?" he asked me.

"She's gone. She's just vanished. I don't know where she
is. She's not at home, and no one can tell me anything."

'He took off his spectacles and rubbed his nose. He used
to do that when he was going to say something he knew you
wouldn't like.

"If I was her father, I would have tried sending her away.
Just to see if that didn't make it wear off."

"It's not going to wear off," I said. "What if they marry her off? What if they beat her?"

"Aman, calm down and think rationally—"

"Did you?" I shouted at him. "Did you?!"

'I slammed the door behind me. My father wrenched it open and shouted down the corridor, "Where are you going?"

'Policemen were snapping to attention, watching us curiously. "To file an FIR. A missing person report," I said.

"Come back here, Aman!" he shouted.

'I walked away without looking back.

'The officer at the desk looked really nervous when he told me he couldn't write the report. "Sahib has asked you to wait."

"Are you going to do your duty or not?" I said, made frantic by my worry for her. "If you refuse to file this report, I shall go to the press."

"Sahib has asked you to wait until he returns," he repeated. "He has gone to meet her father. He said to please go home and wait."

'So, I waited. What I would have given to be at that meeting! My father and hers. A rock meeting a mountain.

'My father came home after a couple of hours. I was sitting at the dining table waiting for him. I had calmed down by then. I pulled some ice cream out of the fridge and silently scooped it into two bowls for us. My way of saying sorry.

"I spoke to her father," he said. "He has sent her away for a while. He doesn't want this relationship."

"What did you say to him?"

"I said that we cannot dictate to our children who they will love. To give both of you time. But he would not listen."

"I knew he wouldn't," I said.

"I knew that too," said my father, "but I had to try. You are my son. This is your happiness."

'We were silent for a while.

'My father spoke carefully. "I got back to my office to find papers on my desk. I have been transferred to Kashmir. Effective immediately."

'That shook me. It had never occurred to me that there would be repercussions for my father.

"What are you going to do?" I asked.

"I have two options," he said. "Resign. Or go."

"Which one are you going to take?"

'My father looked me in the eyes as he spoke. "I understand you love this girl. But you have already been hurt because of it. They beat you up. With me out of the way, I don't know what they would do to you. Come with me."

"You're going?" I said, shocked.

"She is gone for a while. You can do nothing here except wait. Come with me. We will come back."

"No," I said immediately.

"Please," said my father. "You are all I have left. Please, my son. Come away with me. We will come back. Give it time. Let me think of a way. Please."

'We hadn't spoken to each other properly for years. He had never begged me for anything before.

"Do you know where she is?"

"Yes. She is safe. She is not married. She is in her father's village, in her grandmother's house. I have people watching her. I knew this was coming. I am a policeman, you know."

'I was so relieved, I could have wept. "Thank you," I said.

'He looked at me. "I promise you that I will find a way to get you together. I promise that I will have my men keep an eye on her so that she comes to no harm."

"What if he marries her off to someone else?"

"I won't let it happen. I swear. I swear on your mother."

'I knew there was no oath more powerful for my father. I knew there was nothing more I could do for the time being.

'I agreed to come away. To bide my time. I was sure that the love between me and Diya was strong enough to outlast any separation. I thought I would go away for a month. Things would calm down. And my father would work out a plan for us to be together.

'He looked at me. 'Then it happened.'

My brother took him. Three days after he landed in Kashmir, my brother picked him up in broad daylight from the middle of a crowded street. He was the son of the new DGP and a target. Aman came to Kashmir and ended up in a cabin in the middle of the woods, unsure if he was going to live or die.

'I don't know if she is back. I don't know what has happened to her. I know nothing!' he said. 'And she has no idea what has happened to me.'

'I'm sorry, Amanbhai,' I said. I was terrified. I knew how this story ended. Kidnapping stories never ended well. She would never know what happened to him.

He knew too. 'I don't think I will ever see her again,' he said. 'Your brother will not let me live.'

He had put into words the thought in my head. I hadn't expected to become his friend. I hadn't expected to start calling him 'Amanbhai'. I couldn't look at him.

He spoke softly, with irony in his voice.

Is it my fault?
Is it yours?
Blame instead the stars,
That our lives are tied to
With such fragile thread.
Know that all men live,
All men die.

His voice trailed off into silence. He lay down and pulled his blanket over his head.

Fate. It had brought him here, thousands of miles from the girl he loved. Held hostage by men who hated his father. Not knowing what had happened to her. She not knowing what had happened to him.

Blame the stars. Who else can you blame?

Diya

Why is losing someone the only way you learn just how much you loved them?

I knew I loved him. But it was only when he was gone from my life that I realized what it meant to have him in it. Even if we never got a chance to speak or to be together. Just seeing him in college. Watching him from across a room. Walking down a corridor and hearing his voice talking to someone. Just knowing that he was alive and well and somewhere close.

I told myself he loved me. I told myself he would return. His father had taken him away too. But I had this bad feeling. This sensation of falling down that stayed in my stomach, filled my days, and even my dreams.

He was gone and I had nothing left to hold on to to get from one day to another.

So, I sang. I sang all the songs that we had sung together. I closed my eyes and imagined his voice joining mine. My father locked me in a cage, and I sang like a bird.

> The stars you named,
> Became ours forever,
> They watch in a still dark sky.
> The love you named,
> Can leave me never,
> It can never die.

> I will count the stars as I wait for you,
> And make the whole sky ours.
> This world is not enough to hold
> Our love, so we reach for stars.

Kabir

Aman refused to talk about her any more. When I asked, he would change the topic. He began to ask me questions instead. About the home I had left behind. My mother. My father. He had a way of listening that made you talk about things you had buried deep. I told him about my brother and the sixer that changed our lives.

'Have you ever played cricket after that?' he asked.

'No,' I said.

'Come on,' said Aman. 'Let's go play.'

I refused. 'I've never touched a cricket bat again. I don't want to.'

'What happened was an accident. You can't punish yourself by giving up the thing you love the most.'

'My brother suffered for me.'

'Adding your suffering to that won't change anything. Don't give up on something you love so easily.' He was looking at me as he said it. 'Happiness is not so easy to find.'

I shrugged. 'Come on,' he said. 'Let us be happy for a little while.' I felt so sad and guilty that I agreed.

We played cricket under the white trees with a slat of wood and a rubber ball, struggling to see through the falling snow. I refused to bat, so I bowled. Aman batted, and he was awful at it. We laughed so much that snow fell off the trees as the sound echoed around us.

I didn't want to touch that bat, but Aman was so damn inept that I finally had to demonstrate how batting was done. I just meant to show him how, but I touched it and then I didn't want to let it go. Aman bowled, I batted, and we played in the snow until the world turned to twilight and the stars came out. Happiness came back to me, and it had been so long since I had been happy that I couldn't recognize it.

I'm stupid. It didn't strike me till after he was dead that he was playing that badly on purpose.

That night, it stopped snowing. The rumble and thud of lumps of snow falling from the trees ended. Silence descended. It meant my brother would be back soon.

I made a decision. 'You must go back to her, Amanbhai,' I said.

He looked at me with those sad eyes of his. 'I don't think there is much chance I will get out of here alive.'

'No. I won't let them kill you,' I said.

'You may not have much choice in the matter,' he said softly. 'I am a hostage. Your brother hates me. My father is the DGP, and they want to make a point.'

I had decided what I had to do. 'Tomorrow. Tomorrow I'll let you go. Just run away.' It was a betrayal. I was betraying my brother and the cause. But Aman had become a brother too.

'I will if you come with me,' he said softly.

'I can't. I have a cause.'

'Come away with me. Come on. I'll take you to Mumbai. We'll get you in a college. Maybe you'll even find a girlfriend.'

'I can't, Amanbhai.'

But that night I lay awake thinking about going to college in Mumbai. Hanging out with friends. About worrying over nothing more than an exam. About walking into a canteen and ordering a cup of coffee. A simple cup of coffee and all the freedoms it implied.

And I lay awake thinking about her. The girl with a voice like light. But in the end, it came back to my brother. I couldn't leave him. Not after all that he had borne for me. I could not betray him to that extent.

Aman stayed awake too. He was writing something by the light of the lantern. I could hear the rustle of papers. I thought it was a poem. But towards midnight, he said, 'I know you're not sleeping,' and handed me a letter. It had her name on it.

'Why are you giving this to me? Give it to her yourself.'

'I want you to take it to her.'

'But she lives in Mumbai . . .' I began and stopped. Mumbai. A world away from here. A world forbidden to me.

He just looked at me. 'If anything happens, you must take it to her. Promise me you will.'

'Nothing will happen, Amanbhai. You will leave tomorrow. And I won't tell them a thing, I swear. I'll throw them off the trail.'

'Still. Just promise me.'

I made him the promise while the wind sighed and the night lay silent.

'*Mere ma ki kasam*, bhai, I will do it.'

The next morning, I woke him up before there was light in the sky. I had packed a few things.

'Come on, Amanbhai. You have to leave now,' I said. 'It hasn't snowed through the night. I will point you in the right direction. And I will cover the tracks you make as far as I can.'

He looked at the little bundle in my hands. 'No,' he said. 'I won't go. Not unless you come.'

I wasn't expecting that. 'I can't,' I said. 'This is my life.'

'It is not. It is not the life you should be having. It is not even the life you want.'

'I can't go with you,' I said.

'Then I will not go,' said Aman stubbornly.

I argued. I begged. I even used her name to try and get him to leave. 'She is waiting for you, Amanbhai. You can't let her wait.'

'I want you to meet her. I want to take you back with me and say to her, "This is my friend Afzal. He's starting a new life."'

'If you stay here, you will die!'

'No,' he said softly. 'If I leave you here, you will die.'

Such a stupidly stubborn man. At one point I lost my temper and threatened to kick him off the porch. He started laughing. It made me so mad. But how can you stay mad at someone who smiles so teasingly at you? And who only wants to save your life?

I sat down next to him. 'Let's pretend,' he said. 'Let's pretend that we aren't here. That you've come with me. We are in Mumbai.'

'In college,' I said, unable to help joining in.

'In the canteen,' he said, smiling. 'Hanging out. I'm reading a book.'

'What else is new?' I said, rolling my eyes. 'All you do is read poetry.'

'What are you doing?'

'I'm ordering a cup of coffee,' I said slowly. 'And when it comes, I'm going to drink it. One sip at a time. And if I'm lucky, there may be a girl across the room who drinks every sip with me.'

I said it, and it became real. I knew that I would leave. That I would go with him. To Mumbai. To college. He knew too. It was evident in the grin that spread across his face.

'So now what?' I asked.

'Now we have some tea,' said Aman, calmly. 'Then we both leave.'

I was so exhausted with arguing, I didn't protest.

He made strong tea with ginger, and we sat on the porch and drank it. My last cup of tea. My last time on that porch. My heart lifted.

Aman was humming as he drank. I realized what the song was. 'Bombay se aaya mera dost'. I burst into laughter. Then I began to sing with him. We both got up and capered on that porch, singing and dancing in our happiness. Then my voice faltered and stopped.

'What is it?' said Aman.

There were shadows standing under the trees. They moved, and my brother and three men stepped out into the clearing.

'Singing,' said my brother. 'The fucker is singing.'

He ran forward and swung the barrel of his gun, clubbing Aman, who fell from the porch into the snow. His blood was bright against the white ground.

'Bhaijaan! What are you doing?'

'No,' he said, turning to me. 'What are *you* doing? I left you a prisoner. Not a singing companion. This man is our enemy. Not a friend.'

But he had become one. I didn't dare say a word. Aman was getting groggily to his feet. My brother kicked him hard. He fell to his knees and stayed there.

'Do you know what your father did yesterday?' my brother said. Aman said nothing, just watched him warily, blood dripping off the side of his head. 'Do you know what he did?'

I felt my heart sinking. My brother was very angry. I had seen the things he did when he was angry.

'We asked for three men in exchange for you. Instead, your father led a raid on a safe house. He expected to find you there. You weren't. But three of our brothers were, and now they are dead.'

He shoved his face close to Aman's. 'Your father is a murderer. And he must be punished.'

Aman spoke softly. 'I am not responsible for what my father does. I do not believe in violence. I am sorry for your loss. Very sorry.'

'You're sorry? It's going to take more than that.' My brother put his gun against Aman's forehead. 'I am going to deliver you to your father. Dead.'

I jumped from the porch to the ground and stood in front of Aman.

'Bhaijaan, he doesn't believe in violence. He thinks what his father is doing is wrong.'

My brother stepped back and looked from him to me.

'Why do you plead for him?' he asked.

I said, 'He has nothing to do with the police. Or politics. That is just his father.'

'He is an Indian,' spat my brother. 'He is the son of a murderer.'

'He is a good man,' I replied. This made my brother furious.

'A good man?'

'Bhaijaan, please. He is like a brother to me.' I knew I had said the wrong thing. I knew it in the silence. I saw it in the expression on my brother's face—I had signed Aman's death sentence with my words.

My brother put his face close to mine. I could smell the alcohol on him. 'I am your brother,' he said. 'I am the same brother who was in their jails for three years. Who never saw light for three years. Who bore pain. Who bore torture. Who bore everything. For what? For you.'

'I know, bhaijaan,' I said. 'I know. Forgive me.'

'And you have forgotten me for . . . this?'

'No. I can never forget you. Forgive me.'

'Forgive you? When you turn your back on everything that I did for you? When you betray us? Betray me. Betray your own brother.'

'You are my brother. I cannot betray you,' I said.

My brother put the gun in my hands. 'Go on,' he said. 'Prove that you are my brother. Put a bullet through his head.'

The gun was heavy in my hands. I looked at Aman on his knees in front of me. He looked up at me. His face was calm. Almost smiling.

'Shoot him,' said my brother.

Diya

It's time for the next death. The minutes have counted down and I haven't noticed. Everybody has their eyes on the door. Some eyes are sliding over to Kabir. It's his turn.

'Tell me,' I say. 'Tell me before—'

We hear Salim at the door. Kabir looks at me. We have run out of time.

But it is not to our group that Salim comes. He walks past us and into another room. Kabir takes a deep breath and closes his eyes.

On screen, the presenter is wearing a black band. He sombrely announces that they will no longer be telecasting the executions. Instead, they will observe a one-minute silence. He asks the nation to join him. The noise of the television running non-stop suddenly becomes silent. The screen shows the national flag.

We strain our ears in that sudden and unexpected silence. We hear garbled shouts. Screams. Then the unmistakable sound of a single shot. It is followed by a volley of shots. There is silence again.

Somebody hears the sudden silence. Somebody is in this moment. But it is not me. I am lost in darkness. I am lost in a story that I don't want to hear the end of. The minute of silence takes forever to slide past. I count the seconds slowly. I cannot bear for them to end. I cannot bear to hear the end to Aman's story.

The voices on the television set come back. Their horror, their sorrow is shrill in the room. I speak under the cover of the noise.

'And you killed him?' That's not my voice. I don't recognize it.

Kabir opens his eyes. There are tears running down his face as he replies, 'No. I laid the gun at my brother's feet, and with folded hands I begged for Aman's life.'

Kabir

I begged. I grovelled. 'Bhaijaan, let him live. Please.'

'Has he made you mad? Has he turned your mind?'

'No, bhaijaan.'

'His father is the man who orders the bullets. Who kills our children in the streets. Who fills the jails with the innocent.'

'He is not responsible for what his father does. He has not killed anybody.'

'And will we not kill the children of those who kill our children?'

I never thought I would say it. 'An eye for an eye will only make the whole world blind.'

This enraged him. 'Blind? The whole world is blind already! It does not see us. It is deaf. It does not hear us. It does not care for us.'

'Please, bhaijaan. I beg of you. I beg for his life.'

'Shoot him,' said my brother. 'Or you will have betrayed everything we believe in. You will have betrayed me. Shoot him.'

I looked into Aman's eyes. The moment he had talked about had come. 'No, bhaijaan. I will not kill,' I said.

Aman smiled at me. There was blood dripping down his face. He was on his knees facing death. And he was smiling.

My brother picked up the gun and pulled the trigger twice.

One.

Two.

I closed my eyes. I closed my eyes and stumbled away. I heard Aman fall in the snow. I did not turn my head to look back. I couldn't. My tears froze as they fell from my face and lay like diamonds on the ground. In my head I saw Aman, smiling up at me with such pride.

Diya

I don't want to believe it. I don't want to believe what he has come thousands of miles to tell me.

Let this end another way. Let him not be dead. Please. Let there be a miracle and another twist to the story.

Let him not be dead.

His voice is choked with tears. 'I lost two brothers that day. The one that God gave me. And the one I chose.'

His grief is silent. Tears roll down his face, and he makes no sound. Finally, he says, 'I should have kept quiet. I should have not said a word. I opened my mouth and I killed him. I could have saved him somehow, but I didn't.'

Kabir

I fell to my knees in the snow and stayed there. I heard them drag him away. 'We'll dump him at his father's door,' said my brother.

Still, I knelt unmoving in the snow. I heard my brother say, 'Leave that one be. He is no longer my brother. He is a traitor. Let him be. He is nothing to me now. Aazadi does not need traitors.'

I heard them walk away. I could not move. I knelt there until the day bled away into night. Then I got up and began to walk. I never looked back once. I could not bear to see the stain on the white snow.

The snow was falling. I walked on with the darkness thick before my eyes. I was lost in a world of night with no path before me. Everything around me began to vanish. There was nothing left except darkness and bitter cold. I was shaking with my cold and grief. There was no point in carrying on.

I lay down in the snow and looked up at the stars. They were so beautiful.

A house of stars. I'd dreamed of it so often. Drawn it so many times that my mother laughed at me. 'You'll have to put on a roof,' she always said. 'Or the snow will get in.'

And I always asked, 'But then, how will the stars get in?'

I gazed up at the sky and knew that I had finally found the house of stars that every man finds at the end.

Then I heard his voice in my head. 'Get up. You have to get up or you will die.'

I laughed. 'But I want to die, Amanbhai.'

'You cannot,' he said. 'You made a promise you have to keep. You have to find her.'

'She is too far away,' I said. 'The stars are closer. Leave me here. I am going to count them.'

'You called me bhai. You cannot break your promise to me.'

'You are dead, Amanbhai. I want to be with you.'

'No. I need you to be with her. She is alone now. Get up.'

'Please, bhai. It is so peaceful here. No more killing. No more pain.'

'Get up.'

'I hate this world, Amanbhai. People kill other people. I hate it. I won't be part of it any more.' I lay there and told him all about my pain. 'I left my mother and father. Today I left my brother. I lost you. I have no one. The world has taken every scrap of love I ever had. I lost two brothers today. If I stay here, at least I can join one.'

But Aman only said one thing again and again. 'Get up. Keep your promise.'

At that moment, I had a choice. I knew what I wanted with all my heart. I wanted to lie in the snow, peaceful at last. There was such peace alone out there in the woods under the stars, with the snow falling and the world holding its breath. But I had made a promise, and I chose to keep it.

Struggling back to my feet was the hardest thing I have ever done. The snow was still falling as I began to walk, putting one foot in front of the other. Aman stayed with me at every step. We walked together through that long, long night.

After that, he never left me. Not for a moment. It was his voice that gave me courage. That kept me going.

We hid together. We lied and stole food and just kept going. And we talked about love.

'What is the point of your letter? You are gone.'

'I want her to know I loved her. And love never goes away.'

'Lies! Lies!' I shouted. We were on a train. Heads turned to look at the madman talking to himself in the doorway. 'It all goes away. Nothing good stays. Only hate and killing and blood remain.'

'No,' he whispered. 'Love never goes away.'

We were in the back of a truck that was travelling through fields touched with a fuzz of green brought by the spring.

'You're dead. What use is your love?'

'Love is never wasted,' he said.

We were in a deserted bus stand in an unknown town, late at night. 'What is death, Amanbhai?' I asked.

'Knowing you can never again be with the one you love.'

'I have been dead for so many years, Amanbhai,' I said. 'No one has ever loved me.'

We argued and fought and talked. Every step of the long way, he was there. And he led me to her.

Now I am in a mall, waiting to die. And Aman is gone. He left me. He led me to the girl that he loved, and he left me.

'He led me here,' I say. 'From Kashmir to Mumbai is a long way. I came to keep my promise. That was the only atonement that I could make. So, I came to find you.'

She looks at me as if I'm a monster. She looks at me as if I'm telling lies.

'Aman is dead,' says Diya. Her voice is blank.

'Yes,' I say. 'I'm sorry. I am so sorry.'

'And you are a terrorist.'

'They call themselves freedom fighters. I don't call myself anything. I don't want to fight. I don't understand freedom that is built on violence. It took the death of Amanbhai to make me understand that.'

'Aman is dead,' she whispers. There are tears seeping into her voice now.

'Read the letter,' I say. 'I came all the way to give it to you. He made me promise, and I had to keep that promise.'

She looks down at the letter in her hands. Aman's words. The last thing he'll ever say to her.

201

Aman

My beloved Sunshine,

I love you.

My father keeps telling me that I am too young to even understand what love is. I keep telling him that Romeo was sixteen and Juliet was fourteen. I think grown-ups forget what they were like at our age. They don't remember that they knew love.

This is what I know.

That I can tell when you enter a room without looking. That I hear your voice and my heart beats faster. That the first time I saw you, I was lost. That it is you. Only you. You are the one.

I know that I was searching for something. And you are the answer to everything I was looking for. I know that life changed the day I saw you. It bent around the shape of you. And now it will always be different because I have loved you.

The world is a dark thing filled with hate. But your love has been my light. My nights have been lonely. But your love has kept watch with me. My days have been filled with fear, but your love has laughed at my side. You are never away from me. Every moment you are in my heart, in my thoughts. Who can ever separate us? When you live here in my heart.

When you get this letter, I will be gone. But my love will always stay.

I know you will hurt. You will cry. Don't, my beloved. Don't. I could not bear it.

I want you to know that you have been loved. And no one and nothing can take that from you. I want you to remember that each time you feel alone. I want you to remember that each morning. I want you to remember that in the dark nights that never end. I want you to remember that with each cup of coffee you ever drink. You have been loved. As fully, as completely, as one human being is capable of loving another.

Keya Ghosh

You have been loved with all my heart.

I love you. And I always will.

—Aman

Diya

Once, when I was little, I had a little box, all pink and gold with a tiny lock in the shape of a heart. I put all my treasures in it. Whatever treasure means to a six-year-old. Clips, a chewed-up pencil, a shiny bracelet.

Then I decided I was going to fill it with love. I insisted my father put his love in it. That my mother fill it with her kisses. They did so, laughing. Then I closed the box tightly so that I could save that love all my life. But in the morning the box was empty.

It has stayed empty all my life. The older I got, the more I realized that it was empty. My father never really loved me. My mother didn't dare.

The last thing that Aman did was give me a gift. He gave me a treasure box. A box filled with so much love, it is enough to last my whole life.

Kabir

When she looks up from the letter, her eyes are filled with tears.

'I'm sorry,' I say.

She jerks back from the words. Then she snaps. She flings herself on me, slapping me, hitting me. 'Sorry? That's all you've got left to say? You should have saved him! You should have let him run away. You should have saved him!'

I make no attempt to defend myself. I just sit there while she hits me and shouts. I let her rant at me. She's only saying the same things I say every night to myself. I let him die. I know that already. It's a splinter in my heart.

The terrorists drag us apart. They are laughing.

'Lovers' fight?' one of them asks. 'What did you say to her?'

She wrenches herself free. She gets as far as she can from me and curls up like a child. Manu runs to her and puts his arms around her. He glares at me. I watch helplessly. I have to let her cry and do nothing. It hurts.

Why do the tears of those we love hurt us so much? More than if we cried ourselves. She cries, and it is me who is falling apart.

I don't care if I die. I have done the last thing I promised to. Now nothing ties me to this world.

Salim comes back into the room. I stand up. I am ready.

Salim looks from me to her. She is weeping and won't look at me. He bends over Diya.

'What happened? Little tiff? Say goodbye now. He's going to die.'

She turns away. She won't look at either of us.

With one of his sudden changes of mood, Salim is angry. 'He is going to die, woman. All he wants is a kiss before he dies.' He grabs her hair and forces her face around.

'No,' I say. 'Just let her be.' I shudder to think of her lips on mine like this. In hatred and grief and anger.

Salim speaks in a coaxing whisper. 'Don't you want to give him a kiss before he dies? That's all he wants!'

Diya turns her head and spits in my face.

'Women,' says Salim, laughing. 'Unpredictable'. He lets her hair go and she reels back. He turns to me. 'Shall we go?'

I turn for the door. I'm ready to go.

Nobody moves. No one says a word. Then I hear Harish's voice. 'Wait! You have to wait and listen!' He's pointing at the TV screen. The anchor is back on, and her tone is different.

'The spokesman for the government has just made an announcement. The government will meet all the demands of the terrorists unconditionally. A plane will be fuelled up and ready to take off for any destination they choose in forty minutes' time.'

No! I want to scream at her. *Don't shove me back into life again. I've done what I came to do. I have nothing to return to. Don't save me.*

Salim gives an exultant shout. His men mob him, hugging him and slapping each other on the back. I am forgotten. I stand there, stunned. Then I feel someone tugging at my jeans. It's Harish. 'Sit down,' he begs. 'Just sit down.'

I sit.

I sit there, blankly, while a spokesman of the government appears on all the channels simultaneously. He is making an announcement of the demands that the government has accepted. I stare at the screen, not able to hear him, dazed. All I can see is him scratching the side of his nose again and again as he reads. Something keeps nagging at me. This is wrong. This is all wrong.

It is my brother's voice that floats into my head. Just before we did our first 'pickup', he had vanished for three weeks. When he came back, he briefed us about all he had learnt. He taught us to read the official responses. 'Be very sceptical of offers. If they are going to send someone in, first they'll make a generous offer to get you off guard. Everyone gets relaxed. Which means slower reaction times. Less shots get pulled off. More hostages survive.'

I come out of my fog, and my brain works overtime, picking up clues and putting them together. This is classic misdirection. Give the kidnappers a false victory before you move. If they were going to send in a team, they would do it now, when the terrorists were buoyed with a false sense of victory. We were just about to get raided.

I know what I have to do. What Aman would have wanted. I have to get her out of here alive.

'Harish,' I whisper. 'You have to be ready.'

'Yeah, I know. To leave. To get back to our lives. I'm going to be a new man. I'm going to do everything differently, I swear!'

'Listen to me,' I say urgently. 'No one is getting out of here. Not through the front door.'

'What?'

'I think the government is going to send in a commando team to get us.'

'What? Really? What about them meeting the demands?'

'Lies. Lies to distract the terrorists. Get them off their guard.'

His face falls. I have never seen anyone so disappointed. 'Are you sure?' he asks in a small voice. 'Shit! Why doesn't Salim figure that out?'

I look at where Salim is hugging and backslapping his men. 'Arrogance. He thinks he has them by the balls. Fanaticism. He thinks God is on his side. Who knows? Stay alert. And if anything happens, we have to head that way.' I point towards the inside of the store.

'Why? The way out is in the other direction,' he says.

'We'll never make it out from the front entrance. All that glass. That's where they're going to be coming in from. The only thing to do is get farther away. So we don't get shot by mistake. Wait for the army to mop them up.'

I see the hope come back into this face as my words sink in. 'The army! Those dudes know what they are doing.

They'll send in specially trained commandos, right? They'll get us out of here. We are going to get out of here!'

'You have to help me with her,' I say, indicating Diya. He looks over to where Diya sits. She's slumped in her own grief, uncaring of what happens next.

'What's wrong with her? What the hell happened between the two of you? I had such high hopes for you.'

'Just help me get her out of here with us. I won't go without her. And she won't go with me.'

He looks at me sympathetically. 'You've got it bad, man.'

Salim sends one of his men to fetch sweets from the food section. The others hustle all the remaining hostages into the room where we are. They all crowd in fearfully, convinced that one of them is going to be chosen to go through the door next. We are the only ones who have been watching television and know what's going on.

Salim addresses them. 'I thank you for having been with us through this test of our belief and faith. It is now over. The government has agreed to all of our demands.'

The terrorists begin to move through the hostages, handing out sweets. A slow buzz of conversation has started. The idea that it's over is sinking in very slowly.

'We are working out the logistics with the government,' says Salim. 'But you'll be out of here soon.' The buzz gets louder. People are praying, thanking God, exclaiming.

Salim speaks, cutting through the buzz and silencing it. 'Of course, a chosen few will go with us and stay till the end. Just as insurance, so that your government doesn't try anything.' There is a stunned silence. You can see dread seep back into the room as faces fall.

'Shall we begin?' says Salim. And, right on cue, the lights go off. In the darkness, we hear a tortured shriek. It is the sound of metal buckling. They are taking down the front shutters.

There are screams, curses. Above them all, I yell, 'Get on the floor. Down! Now!'

We are all crowded together, and it's chaos. Time seems to slow and stretch, and everything is happening in the same moment.

We can hear smashing. Booted feet. Then, deafening claps of sound and white light blind us. Stun bombs.

There is the sound of shots. Someone is screaming. I crawl over to Diya in the dark. I have to shove people out of my way, climb over tangles of limbs. Harish follows me, grunting. People are running. Tripping over us. There are sudden blinding flashes as the guns fire. It is a nightmare that unfolds around us.

I just keep going until I get the scent of lemons. I am beside her.

'Come on,' I whisper to her. 'We are getting out of here. Come with us.'

But she won't agree to come with us. 'Just leave me here,' she says fiercely. 'DON'T COME NEAR ME.'

'You have to come with us,' I say.

'Come on,' says Harish. 'We're going to get out of here'.

'Leave me alone,' she says. 'Leave me here.'

There is random gunfire, flashes of light. Deafening thuds and smoke. It's disorienting. No one knows what the hell is happening. Flashlights are flickering in the corridor outside. A terrorist screams, 'Stay where you are! Don't move!' He grabs the nearest hostage in the dark. It is Malini. Then we hear him yell. Manu has attacked him, biting and kicking.

'Grab her!' I yell at Harish. He does. We are both trying to drag Diya with us. She fights us, kicking and thrashing.

'Shit! Have you gone mad?' Harish yells at her. 'STOP IT!'

Then, there is an explosion and a blinding flash of light. Glass goes flying everywhere. The terrorists have triggered some of the explosives they have laid.

We are knocked to our knees. Harish falls down and doesn't get up. I let her go and crawl to him. I am almost blind and my ears are ringing.

'Don't be dead. Don't be dead.' I am praying.

He's not dead. But a flying chunk has hit him hard and he's passed out. I try to lift him and can't. I have to choose. Him or her. I leave him lying and run back to her.

She is trying to get back on her feet, dazed. I grab her arm. She fights me.

'Let me be! I want to die!'

My ears are buzzing loudly and I can hear nothing. Then I swallow and the sound comes back. 'So do I!' I shout back. 'I want to die! But I can't. Not until you are safe. Aman won't let me.'

She stops struggling at his name.

I say, 'Don't you understand? I have to save you. I couldn't save him. I have to save you.'

I hold out my hand. 'Please come with me. This is what he wants. Please.'

'He's gone,' she whispers.

'Yes,' I say. 'I would have given my life in his place if I could have.'

'Yes,' she says. 'I would have too.' We look at each other, both mourning for the man we love.

'Let me save you. Please,' I beg.

She looks at my hand. But she won't take it. She shrugs it away and gets to her feet. She nods at me. We run to the door and into the rest of the store.

I have planned the run already. I have been scoping the place out from the moment we were herded in and have worked out a rough plan of the mall in my head. Our best bet is to get as far away from the fighting as we can and then just lie low until the army begins cleaning up. Except, from the sound of it, the operation has gone seriously wrong. There is a series of deafening explosions and flares of light and then a stunned silence. The terrorists have set off the explosives they had laid. I don't think the army was expecting it.

I can hear booted feet but they sound like they are retreating. The gunfire starts up again. But now it is the terrorists' guns that speak again and again. The rescue operation has unravelled in a few seconds.

We turn and run away from it, into the heart of the store. I point and we run up the stalled escalators. We find ourselves in a giant signature shop and just keep going. We run down long, dark aisles loaded with things, shoving aside shopping carts. We stop, winded, somewhere in the clothing section.

I gesture and we both slide into a long row of hanging garments and crouch there, listening.

We hear a confused babble. Men's voices shouting. A scream. A single shot. And then the voice of the person I was hoping had been shot to hell. Salim Mukhtar. He is yelling. He's screaming. 'Find the hostages who have run away. Find them now!' So, others have run as well.

I grab her arm, and without a word we move farther, deeper, creeping along as carefully as we can. 'He's alive,' she says. 'He won't let us live.'

'He won't find us.'

'He'll just blow the place apart,' she says.

And like an echo we hear Salim's voice. 'Lay the rest of the explosives. If we go, we will take this whole place with us,' he is yelling. 'We will take them all with us! This will be our *kabar*! Our martyr's monument!'

We stand there listening, frozen in place. 'Run!' I say. 'Let's get as far away as we can.'

I plunge into the darkness, then stop. She has not moved. She is just standing there. 'It's no use,' she says. 'They are going to blow the place up. We are going to die.'

I try to slow my breathing down. To stop my heart from hammering. This is it. We both stand there, just waiting.

Then, I don't know from where, a thought comes into my head. I am not going to die like this. Terrified. Like a rat in a trap. I'm not.

'Come on,' I say. 'Dying is the last thing we're going to do. Let's do it our way.' I look around. The army has cut off the electricity, but a few backup emergency lights have kicked in. But they are few and scattered and leave great areas of darkness between them. I can make out we're in the signature store of a clothing brand.

I begin to grab clothes off the rack. 'I've never worn a suit. What do you want to wear?'

She stares at me for a moment like I'm crazy.

'I am going to die,' I say. 'In a few minutes. I'm cramming in whatever experiences I can.' I hurriedly put on the jacket.

Diya just looks at me.

'Come on,' I say. 'This is all the time we have.'

Diya nods. Then she jumps up and begins to pull things off the racks as well. 'I need shoes,' she says. 'Stilettoes.'

We find shoes. We pull jewellery and clothes off the mannequins. We race each other to the changing rooms.

The changing rooms are side by side. I pull my clothes off frantically. I can hear Salim ranting. All other sounds have stopped. His voice carries over to us clearly. Someone screams.

I don't care. I'm crazy. I'm high. I'm laughing at the sadness and the madness of it. In the other changing room, I can hear her laughing too. We're both breathless with excitement. There is only this moment. Only us. And we are alive right now.

We come out of the rooms and look at each other. She is wearing a long dress. One shoulder is bare. She looks beautiful.

'You look like a heroine.'

'You look pretty good yourself.'

We stare at each other, suddenly self-conscious, but still on a high.

'And now what?' she asks. Her lip trembles. The elation leaves her.

I don't want to lose her in these last few minutes. I improvise desperately to hold on to the moment. 'Now we're shooting a movie. You're the heroine. I'm the hero. This is the bit where they meet for the first time.'

She says, 'They're at a party. He asks her to dance.'

I hold out my hand. 'She says "yes".'

She takes my hand.

'Come on,' I say. 'Let's get to where there's more place.' We walk to where there is empty floor space and a display of mannequins. I spin her around, and her dress flares around her.

She spins back towards me and looks me straight in my eyes. She locks her eyes with mine and doesn't look away. 'He puts his arms around her.'

I do that. Her dress is sort of silky. Her body is warm through it. The smell of lemons is still in her hair. 'The music begins to play,' I whisper.

She begins to sing softly. It is the first time I hear her sing. Her voice is a sunbeam in the dark. It is sunlight at dawn. It is the stars coming out at night.

The stars you named,
Became ours forever,
They watch in a still dark sky.
The love you named,
Can leave me never,

It can never die.

I will count the stars as I wait for you,
And make the whole sky ours.
This world is not enough to hold
Our love, so we reach for stars.

The automatic sprinklers suddenly come on, spattering us with water. More explosions must have gone off in this part of the mall. I start to laugh. This is the ultimate movie moment. We are dancing in the rain. We sway together.

She puts her head against my chest. Where she can hear my heart beating. I whisper a happy ending in her ear.

'Boy meets girl. They fall in love and run away together. Far away. They build a house they can live in together. The floor is made of moon silver. The walls are woven of branches. And the roof is made of the sky. It is a house of stars. They lie in each other's arms in the dark, and they name the stars one by one because they are making a new world. A world where the stars have not yet been named. Where there is no religion. People don't do terrible things to each other. A world that has place for love.'

She sways in my arms, both of us dreaming of the house of stars where we would be safe from the world.

Then she whispers, 'I love him. There is a part of my heart that will always be his. I will never love anyone like I love him.'

'I know,' I say.

She closes her eyes. Then she puts her lips against mine.

Diya

I close my eyes and I kiss him. I know it is the last thing I am going to do. I am going to die, and it is the right thing to do. We both go very still. We wait. Lips just touching, hearts hammering. Waiting.

And then I hear Salim's voice. He's calling my name. My real name. He sounds like he is right beside us. I go rigid in shock.

I break apart from Kabir. How is he here? How does he know? *How does he know?*

'Come on, Surabhi. I know who you really are. I found an ID lying on the floor. And I know who you are.'

The identity card I had shoved into my churidar. He's very close. He's found our discarded clothes. He's found it. It has my father's name on the back. He knows who I am.

'GOD IS GREAT,' his voice sounds as if he is standing right beside us. 'I asked God to give me something to get my people out of here,' he shouts. 'And he gave me you.'

'Run,' I whisper. *We have to run!*

But we don't run. We back away from the voice as carefully as we can, making no noise. Breathlessly we move away, then faster and faster. Away from that voice that is shouting my real name.

We duck down different aisles. Then we spot the toilets ahead of us. Kabir pulls open the closet that holds the brooms. We both squeeze in and shut the door. Through the slits in the door, we can see the bathroom. Nothing moves.

We can hear Salim, but he is heading in another direction. He is shouting my name. 'Come out,' he says. 'I won't harm you. I swear it. You're too valuable to hurt. You and I are going to walk out of here together. Come on.'

Kabir puts his lips against my ears. 'Who are you?' he asks.

I can't lie any more. I have to tell him. 'My name is Surabhi Thakur. My father is Bhai Thakur.'

Kabir

It all makes sense now. Aman always refused to tell me who her father was. I thought he was a rich businessman. Instead, it turns out he deals in the business of hate.

'My father leads a party that thinks India should be only for the Hindus. My father thinks the only good Muslim is a dead one. My father has led riots. He's been indicted by a court three times. He's never gone to jail.'

Her voice is the smallest whisper in my ear. 'Do you hate me now?'

'No,' I whisper back. 'You didn't choose your father. You don't choose the hatred you inherit. You can only choose not to be a part of it.'

'I would rather die than be a part of it,' she says. 'I hate my father and everything he stands for.'

We sit there listening to Salim bellow her name. He is heading away from us.

She shivers. 'If he finds us—'

'We can't let him get you. He'll kill you.' I hold out my hand. She takes it. She is not just giving me her hand. She is giving me her trust. 'Come on. We have to get to the windows. We can smash a window and jump out.'

She is scared to leave the closet. In the darkness, there is a sense of safety. But I know we can't hide for long. He will find us. We have to get to a window.

Diya

It's a nightmare. A game of hide-and-seek that ends in death. We sneak along, trying not to make any noise. We slide along the wall. The first window we find has an iron grill on it. We keep going. It's a long way to the next window. He holds my hand. I cling to it.

We reach the next window and realize our fate is sealed. It too has a grill. Every window has a grill. We are not going to be able to get out. Only the show windows on the ground floor are glass. And Salim Mukhtar is between us and those windows.

Kabir just hangs on to my hand. 'There has to be a way. There has to be a way!' he keeps saying as he searches desperately. He knows as well as I do that once Salim gets his hands on me, there is no hope.

We search and search. So many sections. So many doors. Corridors. And no windows that can let us out.

We find ourselves back at the bathroom, doubling back on our tracks. Kabir looks at the door to the closet. We climb back in, and Kabir shuts the door. It's an admission that there is nowhere for us to go. We can't get away.

We wait in the darkness. I close my eyes and lean against him. He puts his arms around me, and we wait. There is nothing to be said. The minutes tick by. He puts his lips against my ear and whispers. 'I will be waiting for you in the house of stars. Far away from other people's hate.'

Then the bathroom door slams open. Salim comes in with a gun in his hand. We can hear him kicking open the bathroom cubicles. He slams them one by one, and each one sounds like a gunshot. It sounds like he is about to leave when everything goes silent. Kabir turns so that he is shielding me with his body.

The door flies open.

One.

Two.

Two bullets thud into Kabir. He falls. And I am standing there, screaming. Salim reaches out and grabs me by the hair. I stumble over Kabir, and then I am being dragged away from him. I try to go to Kabir but he won't let me.

I am screaming as he drags me away. Kabir is lying on the floor, so still, blood pooling underneath him. I am screaming his name.

Kabir

I am lying on the floor. There is just so much blood. It's all over the place. It takes me some time to understand that it is my blood. I try to get up, but I feel so heavy. I can't. I just can't.

'Get up. You need to get up.' Aman's voice is loud in my ear. 'You need to get up now and go find her.'

He is back. Aman is back. I open my eyes with such effort and see him looking down at me. He is kneeling beside me. 'Come on,' he says. 'Get up.'

Bloody Hindi films. All full of shit. The hero takes dozens of bullets and keeps going. In real life, a couple of bullets and you're on the floor with feet that won't listen to you. I roll over and it is so painful I almost pass out. I can't get up. I begin to crawl.

I crawl in the direction that I last heard her scream. I am trying not to scream in pain myself.

There is a man lying on the floor. He is dead. He is still holding his gun. One of the terrorists. God. There is so much blood. I don't want to crawl through it but there is no way around it.

'Pick up the gun,' says Aman.

I begin to laugh. 'You're telling me to pick up a gun? You're the guy who loves Gandhi.'

'Do something. She's going to die if you don't do something.'

'What can I do that won't end with violence?'

I know this is ridiculous. I've been shot. I'm bleeding. This is not the time to be having a philosophical argument with someone who is inside my head. But I can't help it. I feel like I'm outside this moment, calmly looking in. It's all unreal.

'Save her,' says Aman. 'And don't betray me and all I believed in.'

'How?' It is an impossible task. I don't know how I can do it. I only know that I have to.

I pick up the gun. I check it with hands that are slippery with blood. It still has four bullets in it.

I hear Diya scream. It's away to the right. It gets me off all fours. With a desperate effort, I manage to get to my feet. The gun is a weight that drags me off centre.

I head for the sound. I am reeling, staggering like a drunk man. Holding on to whatever I can to stay upright. That damn gun is so heavy it's dragging my arm down. My knees buckle, and I fall several times. Each time he gets me up and going. He whispers, urges me on. 'You have to find her. You have to keep going.'

'I'm sorry,' I say to him. 'I fell in love with her. I couldn't help it.'

'I know,' he says. 'It's all right.'

'You're not mad?'

He smiles sadly at me. 'I couldn't help falling in love with her. How can I be mad with you for doing it?'

There are no more screams from Diya. No more sounds. I know I'm close but I can't locate her. And the only advantage I have is surprise. All the rest is a mess. I stop and listen.

'He's going to hurt her. He's going to kill her. Find her.'

'I'm trying. I'm trying.'

The area the last scream came from is the toy section. I stumble towards it. Then I hear her crying. Desperate, hopeless sobs. The sound wakes me up. Makes me focus. I also, finally, have a fix on where she is.

I hear Salim's voice. He is yelling on the phone. 'Tell Bhai Thakur I have his daughter! I want him on the phone. I want him to hear every scream. She's going to do a lot of screaming. Unless you play straight with me this time.'

'Save her,' says Aman. 'Please.'

'I will save her. And I will save your truth as well,' I say.

I step around the end of the aisle and I see them.

I point the gun at Salim. He has no idea I'm coming. He's on the phone, screaming demands. He has her beautiful hair wrapped around his arm and is holding her by it. His gun is held awkwardly beside the phone.

I think of all those times I practised with my brother's gun in the quiet woods. I think of myself shooting round after round, wishing I could kill the men who took my brother and returned a stranger. I think of the target in the woods. Think of the target. Think only of the target.

One.

Two.

I shoot him through both kneecaps. He falls heavily to the ground. His gun goes flying out of his reach. Diya shoves his weight off her and scrambles away from him. He is screaming. A high-pitched scream like a woman. She grabs his gun and then looks confused. She doesn't know how to use it and I am too far away. She holds it like a club and hits him across the head. The screaming stops.

I take a step towards her and fall. The world begins to break into pieces.

She rolls me over. She is saying my name, but I don't look at her. Over her shoulder I can see Aman. He is smiling.

Diya is holding my hand. Talking to me. Her voice fading and returning. Time is flowing around us. Fading and returning. The light is fading and returning. And me, fading and returning. Returning with more difficulty each time.

'Stay with me,' Diya whispers. 'You have to stay with me. You can't go. You can't leave me.'

Me, fading, fading, fading.

Darkness begins to lie thick on everything in front of my eyes. I'm starting to get cold. So very cold. I understand why. I'm lying in snow.

The sky above me is dark. An icy wind is blowing. I'm back in the woods again, waiting to die. Silence and snow and cold. It's so peaceful.

Aman is beside me again, like he was last time. 'You have to go back,' he says.

But I don't want to. I am so tired. It will be so easy to just lie here forever.

'You have to love her for both of us. Live for both of us,' he says. I lie there looking up at the dark sky, wondering why there are no stars in it.

He kneels beside me and whispers in my ear, 'Go. She is waiting. *Khuda hafiz.*'

'Khuda hafiz, Amanbhai,' I whisper back.

And he is gone.

Something falls on my face. It can't be snow. It's burning hot. I hear a voice. 'Come back. You can't die! I won't let you.'

It's her voice. That's not snow on my face. It's her tears. Stars begin to appear in the sky one by one. Great wheels of them light the dark. I can see again. I see her kneeling beside me.

I feel her breath on my face. 'It's over. Can you hear them? It's the army announcing we should come out. Please don't let go now.'

I try to speak but it is so difficult. I can't say what I want to. That she is the most beautiful girl I've seen. That I don't want to leave her.

She whispers brokenly to me, 'You can't go. We still have to build a house of stars.'

A house of stars where the door is open for everyone. Where the rooms are filled with love. And the roof is a sky full of stars. Each one holding a wish.

I have to hold on. I have to believe it. We will build our house of stars.

One day we will.